Becoming Michael

Becoming Michael

By Nino Balistreri

Cover: Griffon Studio Arthouse

National Library of Canada Cataloguing in Publication

Caruso, Anthony, 1944-

Becoming Michael / Nino Balistreri

ISBN 978-1-7750849-3-8

Fiction > Gay

Coming of Age fiction

Acknowledgments

I would like to thank good friends and expert helpers.

Bob Turner, a retired educator who witnessed me agonizing over a long list of titles on my white board. The more I came up with, the less I liked.

He offered to look at my draft to see if a name popped out. On reading my story he announced that it was clear to him, it should be called "Becoming Michael". I was overjoyed!

My editor Susan Hoover who taught English Lit has been invaluable to help me keep my story flowing and as always, to correct my drastic punctuation skills.

I also want to thank my graphic designer Rob of Griffin Studio Arthouse for his creativity in cover design.

Good friends with clear heads are always a great help.

1

Mike Nicholas wandered from room to room. He was in total wonderment, viewing his new surroundings. It was difficult to grasp the reality and shock of how this all came about. His emotions were running so strong; they were almost causing him to buckle at the knees. There was just too much to absorb at once

This was a world and an existence that he had never been exposed to. He could not, at this early stage in his life, anticipate being the owner and master of his own kingdom. Being a university student, Mike had yet to even dream of having an apartment, let alone a beautiful home of his own. As he moved around, he had to stop every few steps. His head was swimming because he was holding his breath.

Mike grew up in what he believed, at least when he was little, to be a more or less happy home. The more was certainly thanks to the love and nurturing of his mother. The less was definitely the doing of his stern and hateful father. Other than during school hours, Mike had no close friends. His parents didn't move in a social circle.

That would have provided him with family friends his age. It also would have made him aware at a younger age that his family was far from normal. He had no idea that other parents had happy gatherings of friends and family in their homes. Or that the fathers of most families actually took part in the raising and activities of their sons and daughters.

In grade five Mike's teacher had his own family. He enjoyed telling his class about adventures that they had, while camping and other outdoor activities. Mike's favorite memory was of an event with his teacher's five year old son. His teacher had taken his family to a state park campground for a long weekend. On one afternoon, his wife and daughter left the campsite ahead of them to swim in the campground pool. He got his son into his bathing suit and then changed into his own swim suit. While he was changing, his son had wandered out of the tent ahead of him. As he approached the outside tent flap he was stunned by an amazing sight. His son was standing just a few feet from the tent, talking to and petting the nose of a baby fawn. He quietly backed into the tent, grabbed his camera and photographed the scene. When he told his class the story, he passed copies of the picture to the head of each row of desks, so that they could all look at the snapshot and pass it on.

Strangely to Mike, when his teacher talked about family adventures and points of interest like state parks, Mike could see that his classmates were keen. He didn't understand why. His classmates even talked about going with their parents and siblings to hamburger restaurants. Other than eating lunch out with his uncle Joshua, Mike had never set foot in a restaurant of any kind. Near the end of June that year, his teacher pulled down State and US maps.

He asked each student to come up and tell the class about their plans for the summer. If it meant travel adventures out of state, he wanted them to point the place out on the wall map. As each classmate stepped up, his teacher gave them a pointer to use on the maps. Unknown to the class it was an impromptu exercise in geography.

Some of his classmates were going to actually travel by aeroplane or train. Mike thought that it would be amazing to fly, or go on a train. Others were going to a summer camp where you stayed for a week or two. Mike had no idea what that would be like. Others still were going to visit grandparents and, amazingly, several were going with their parents on road and camping trips just to explore, or in some cases to visit family that lived a long way away. Others still were going to enjoy stay-at-home vacations that included outdoor activities as a family unit.

When his teacher realized that Mike was the only student that had not raised his hand to speak, thinking that he was just being shy, he asked Mike to come forward. Mike just stood there holding the pointer. He looked at the wall maps and then looked at his classmates. Finally he gathered enough resolve to speak. "I have a grandmother. She is my mother's mother. She lives in another state, I'm not sure which one. I just remember that she came to visit two or three times when I was little. I know that my grandfather died before I was born.

"My father has parents that I guess would also be my grandparents, but he never talks to them and they have never come to visit. I am not sure if he doesn't like them, or they don't like him. I think that they are still alive, I get a card from them with a gift certificate for the book store, every Christmas and on my birthday.

I don't know where they live. We have never gone to visit them. This summer I will be at home and swim every day in our neighbors pool. Jayne is a nice lady. She lets me use her pool every afternoon." Mike was aware enough not to mention arts camp to his class. The real danger of his dad finding out laid all too heavily on his mind.

Back at his desk, Mike thought, 'Mom travels with Jayne to see Jayne's mom at least three times a year. Every spring, summer and fall. I wonder where Jayne's mom lives? Maybe I should ask her if I can come along in the summer. I have never been on a road trip. But then I would miss a week of art. I better not; I don't want to miss my art camp. I remember, because when she goes away she leaves all my breakfast and lunch supplies wrapped in the fridge. I get my own cereal and toast in the morning and make my own sandwich for lunch. I don't know what dad eats, he always comes home after supper and goes right to his den. Mom always looks so happy when she returns. Its worth being lonely for a week to make her happy. She is so sad most of the time'.

2

Mike believed that on the whole, Southeastern New Hampshire was a good place to be a kid. His school was modern and the teachers interesting. Mike was a good student, one that every teacher enjoyed working with.

He was an only child. At times Mike thought that life could have been easier if he had siblings. It certainly would have taken his dad's focus off him and his personality. A rough and ready, husky brother who liked hunting and fishing would have occupied all of his dad's attention and left Mike to enjoy, in safety, both his life and his likes.

His father never cared for or paid attention to Mike, at least not in a loving or positive way. From early on, he sensed that Mike was not at all the kind of son he wanted or could ever be proud of. As a little tyke he was too tiny and frail. He easily caught any cold or flu that went around the school. When he was ill in bed his mother gave him loving care. He never once laid eyes on his father till he was well and up again. Mike sometimes thought that his father would be happier if he died from his illness. Then his dad would no longer be ashamed of having him for a son.

His dad was tall and husky, the total opposite in every way. Mike stayed extremely slight in stature till well into his teenage years. By the time he finally grew in body mass, height and strength, his father had long given up on him being worthy of his interest.

There were continual times over the years, when his dad had too many drinks under his belt. When this happened, he would often stare ominously at his son, trying to decide if Mike was actually his biological offspring. It went totally against his "vision of manhood", to admit to fathering such a puny and sensitive boy child. Both Mike and his mom knew from painful experience to give his dad lots of space when he drank and especially for Mike to keep a low profile by mostly staying in his room.

Mike displeased his father right from early childhood. He had little or no interest in his dad's passion for sports, fishing and hunting. Every time his father brought home fresh caught fish or dead birds, and twice to his horror a deer carcass, he refused to go near or touch them. This always brought on rage from his father, but Mike didn't care. His dad could scream and threaten all he wanted. Mike wanted nothing to do with outdoor roughhousing activities, or especially anything to do with the horror of dead carcasses. There was no way that his dad could ever convince him to go out there, to kill these beautiful creatures. When these killings that his father brought home were served up for a meal, it was guaranteed to be a traumatic scene.

Mike refused to eat the wild game. In true fact he loved all kinds of foods. Mike was not a fussy eater. He loved every type of meat, fowl or fish that his mom bought and cooked. But just knowing that his hateful and cruel dad had taken great joy in killing the poor creatures, made it revolting and evil in his mind. Each time this happened his dad would send him to his room in a rage, refusing him an alternate supper.

Mike learned at a young age to wait a while to be safe and sure that his dad was not on the way to his room, to further berate or physically punish him. There were no limits to his rage, especially when it was all too often fueled by a few drinks. Mike knew that to further infuriate his father would end up in a severe beating. Then, on those occasions, once Mike felt that it was safe, he would look deep into the back of his closet.

In anticipation of what usually happened, his mother had each time stashed a small bag lunch with a container of milk in the closet. To be extra safe from discovery, Mike would always close himself into the darkness of his closet to eat his food while keeping his ear sharp for the sound of his door latch opening. He knew also to wait till the next morning after his dad left for work, to bring the empty milk carton and lunch wrappers out to his mother for disposal.

On these occasions, as on many others, his mom sympathized with Mike, but could not stand up in his defense. There was always the real fear of violent reprisals for him and his mom, at the hands of his dad.

His dad's kingdom was his den. He spent most of his time at home in there. Mike knew from when he was little that the den was off limits to him. His dad kept the door closed at all times. That suited Mike just fine. He had no interest in entering his dad's domain. On the rare occasion that the door was open, Mike would not even dare a glance in there. He knew what he would see if he did. In full view, hanging on the wall were the mounted heads of the two deer that his dad had murdered. Mike looked closely at them only once when he was six. His dad was at work and he had followed his mom into the den as she vacuumed and dusted. That day he ended up in his room crying. He believed that they looked so sad to be dead. It was like they were pleading with him, "Why did your father kill me? I was so happy living in the forest." Mike remembered his teacher's picture of his little son petting the baby deer. He so wished that he could see those poor dead deer on his father's den wall happily running in the wild.

3

The two things that Mike truly loved in his existence were school and art. Every summer, recognizing his needs, his mother enrolled him in an art day camp. They did have outdoor sessions to sketch scenery, but most of the classes took place in a large studio space. Enrolling Mike in art camp was a dangerous thing for her to do. Mike learned from the beginning that it had to be their secret. She told his dad that it was a day camp designed around enhanced computer skills and academic advancement. He balked each year, trying to deny approval, due to the cost. It was not about being poor, but rather about wasting his money on a useless son that he was ashamed of, a son that could never live up to his manly standards, or please him by sharing his outdoor likes.

Each summer Mike's mother had to explain it by telling him, "Because of Mike's excellent grades, he qualifies for a scholarship to attend the summer enhancement program." It was an easy lie for her to pull off. Her husband had never even glanced at his son's school work or report cards through the years. All he ever wanted to know was the end result every year. It was not from fatherly interest that he wanted this information, but rather for reference in planning the career that he had chosen for the boy. Only the final grades and advancement mattered; Mike's likes or personal needs did not. His dad's controlling overran every aspect of their lives.

His plan was to control his son's career by forcing Mike to work under him. He intended to bleed out every penny that he had wasted on his disappointing son, both on his upbringing and his education. Having Mike trapped in his office was his plan for maintaining control. He would in the end dominate Mike's life and finances, just as he does his wife's, by keeping her at home, totally dependent on him financially.

The fact that the summer program was not costing him out of pocket removed the possibility of refusal by Mike's father. He had no choice but to give in telling her, "If the brat wants to do it, what should I care, especially if it's not costing me money. Just keep him out of my hair for the entire summer. I have fishing trips planned with my real male friends most weekends."

Mike's father found it strange that a boy his age would rather spend most of the summer in a school setting, even if it was a day camp. What he did not know was, that his wife had avoided any paperwork that he might see by having Mike's uncle Joshua secretly pay all of the costs involved.

Joshua was as unlike Mike's dad as any man could be. The fact that they were blood brothers was truly amazing. Not one ounce of their physical being or mind set suggested that they were related. Mike's dad grudgingly tolerated his brother, but like his disappointing son, he had nothing in common with him.

Mike's mom had no family nearby to rely on for moral or financial support. She had come from the Oregon coast and had met his dad at college. She could only really confide in and trust her neighbor and best friend Jayne and her husband George. Jayne and her husband were the only people in the community who were fully aware of the tyranny and abuse that she and Mike were forced to live with.

From the start, on that first summer, Mike learned the routine. At the end of every camp day he would dutifully drop off his art projects at Jayne's house, before swimming laps in her pool for an hour. Then he came home with his wet bathing suit and towel. Hanging these out should his dad care to take notice, cemented the rouse that he had spent the day at a summer camp. Each morning his mom had a habit of going to Jayne's for coffee. She viewed Mike's artwork then.

Mike assumed that she had always discarded it, rather than chance bringing it home. It would not be safe for him or his mom to have his dad discover what he was really doing with his summer.

As the summers progressed, Mike advanced in his artistic abilities. By the time he was twelve he entered a new phase. At the suggestion of his instructors, rather than the arts camp, he was enrolled in the City Arts College Summer Youth Program. This he truly loved. It involved serious study and hard work for a boy his age. All but one other of the participants in his class was one to three years older than Mike.

At one point in the summer, the college course covered Life Form. Mike was as excited as any young teenager to be drawing nude models. Unfortunately because of the youth of many students, both the male and female models wore brief bathing suits. Mike enjoyed drawing the curves of the females but he was totally fascinated by the males. He was used to seeing the classic and modern nude paintings at the art gallery and private gallery showings that he attended with his uncle Joshua. He didn't understand why the models for his class needed to be covered.

His dad, always completely wrapped up in his own world, paid little or no attention to Mike's comings and goings. As each summer progressed, Mike helped his mother perpetuate their secret, by faithfully swimming his laps in Jayne's pool every day after classes. That way he gained a reasonably good tan. Not that his dad would pay attention to his sons condition, but his mom was worried. There was always the danger that his dad would notice if Mike was pale, in spite of spending his days at 'summer camp'.

4

Growing up, the other joy in Mike's life had been the monthly visits of his uncle Joshua. Mike worshiped his uncle. He was his dad's younger brother and only sibling. They went to parks, galleries, the science center and the zoo, anywhere that Mike wanted to go. Joshua loved spending his evenings playing board games with Mike and his mom. Those were definitely happy evenings filled with great amounts of laughter and love.

His dad always retreated to his den and shut the door so that their laughter would not disturb his watching the sports channels. He did his very best to ignore them all. He made no bones about not liking his own brother. He never showed interest in activities that Mike liked. His attitude was that it had to be his way or no way. That meant sports, hunting and fishing. As his dad often preached at him, "Real activities that makes a man."

The older Mike got the more he enjoyed going to museums, galleries and the science center with Uncle Joshua. On most weekends, they would go to new art openings at private galleries on

Saturday. Uncle Joshua somehow always had actual invitation cards for entrance to these closed events. Mike had no idea how or why this continually happened. He was just happy that it did.

It was as if they actually knew ahead of time that Joshua would be bringing his nephew. While the adults were being served Champagne, they always had a ready supply of Ginger Ale or Seven-up for Mike to sip from his own real champagne flute. No other adults brought children to these events. Mike loved this; it made him feel like he was grown-up and important.

Then, on Sundays, they often spent the day at the city gallery to top their weekend off. Mike loved sitting in the gallery courtyard, to enjoy a late lunch. The food was both strange and exceptionally tasty. While he and Joshua ate, they talked about the art work that they had seen and made plans for Joshua's next visit. Mike loved the way Joshua spoke to him. He always spoke to Mike like an adult. His mom, although loving, just talked to him like a little boy. His dad either ignored him, or mostly snarled, screamed and commanded.

While his mom was loving towards him and free with her hugs, Mike grew up never knowing the feeling that he would have, if his dad actually called him, "Son" or god forbid ever touched him affectionately or hugged him. The only physical contact that Mike experienced from his dad was the all too frequent blows given in rage.

Uncle Joshua had infinite patience and lavished love on Mike. He always gave Mike his undivided attention, taking care to answer every question. He loved explaining things to Mike in great detail as they went along.

14 Nino Balistreri

Mike was so starved for recognition from his father that a simple event one Sunday when he was eight stuck in his mind for years. That Sunday afternoon, when they reached the parking garage near the gallery, it was barricaded off. A bold sign announced, "Closed for concrete repairs". Joshua had to park several blocks away.

The traffic was heavy that day. As they approached the gallery, they had to cross a major intersection. It frightened Mike; trucks and cars were screaming by. Just as the walk signal lit up, Joshua reached down and firmly gripped Mike's hand to guide him safely across the street. It felt so amazing to be held, even by his hand, that Mike wished that his uncle would not let go once they were safely across and back on the sidewalk near the gallery.

In the gallery, Joshua was greeted by the gallery owner and the exhibiting artist. He didn't see what Mike did. Looking at his hand and still feeling the strength of Joshua's grip, Mike pressed his hand into his cheek. He then grasped his rib cage. He fantasized what it would feel like if his dad ever touched or hugged him in a loving and protective way, the way that Joshua did. The only bodily contact that he had ever experienced from his father was from being hit or beaten.

Through these early years, Mike believed that his Uncle Joshua was all knowing, loving and wise. He completely idolized him. His father was brutal and cold, but not just with him. He treated Mike's mom like a servant. She was never allowed a say in matters. His dad brow beat her into submission over every major decision. On occasion when she would try to stand up for herself and voice an opinion, his dad would scream her down and belittle her, opinion on any given matter. These tantrums were always backed with the real threat of violence.

He considered himself as being smart enough to know all. He therefore had the authoritative word on every subject and family decision. He was all rules, demands and sternness, a man to be constantly feared. It took little to bring the fury of his wrath down upon them.

5

In spite of the tensions at home, there was a silver lining. Mike's life, being continually enhanced by his Uncle Joshua. He only had to avoid crossing his dad's path on a daily basis. It was important for him and his mom to keep a low profile when his dad was home. The threat was multiplied on the evenings and weekends when his dad got into the drinks.

Things were always touch and go, but Mike and his mom managed to survive and took their blows when they happened. Mike was now almost eleven and beginning to feel good about himself in spite of his dad's demeaning attitude. He monitored the calendar for Uncle Joshua's upcoming weekends.

During one visit Joshua made a suggestion at supper on Saturday night. He invited them all to spend a weekend the following month at his home on the Cape. Mike was thrilled. He had never actually wondered about where Joshua lived. He just knew that Joshua didn't live nearby. Seeing his excitement at the suggestion, his father immediately yelled at him to calm down. He told Joshua, "My weekends belong to me alone. I make the money around here and I earn my time off. I have no plans that would allow wasting a weekend of my time for a lame visit to the boring Cape."

Hearing this ultimatum, Mike's mom had an idea. Without thinking first, she spoke up and suggested, "You would not have to give up a weekend. Mike and I could drive down to the Cape alone to visit Joshua for a weekend." That was obviously a mistake. Mikes dad immediately flew into a rage, stood up, swore at her and raised his hand in a threat to swing.

As fast as he did so, Joshua yelled, "No". That refocused his attention and made him realize that if he hit her, his brother would be a witness. He sat down with a sullen look on his face and remained silent for the rest of the meal. As soon as he finished eating he rose from the table, gave everyone a nasty look and then shut himself up in his den for the rest of the evening.

No more was ever said about visiting the Cape. Joshua went home Sunday evening with a promise to return in a month. This usual routine took place for two more months without incident. Then one weekend, Mike's entire world shattered and changed. That Saturday night after a full day at the science center with Uncle Joshua, Mike sank into a happy peaceful sleep. He was looking forward to spending Sunday at the city gallery.

A while later Mike was awakened by noises. Creeping to his bedroom door, he could hear loud angry voices. It was Uncle Joshua and his dad arguing. Mike could not hear what it was about without opening his door. He decided that it would be dangerous to do so. His door was too near and in full sight of the living room. Occasionally he could hear his mother's voice cutting in. Every time she spoke up, his dad screamed at her. As always, in fear for her physical safety, she immediately stopped.

Mike sat crouched in a tight ball, on the floor by his bedroom door. He was completely terrified. He knew from experience, when his dad screamed at him or his mom that way, he knew that things were going to be very bad for them. After a while, Mike heard what sounded like a ruckus followed by the front door slamming. He then heard his dad scream at his mom followed by her footsteps running past his bedroom door. By then he was in tears from fright. Then suddenly the house went quiet. He listened for a while longer. Hearing nothing more, Mike thought that whatever the argument was, it was over. He hoped that everything would be back to normal.

Mike knew that he and his mom both lived in fear, of the all too real violence. His dad's hand was often in the air, threatening to bear down on him or his mom. Many times over the years, both Mike but especially his mom bore the marks of his dad's rage.

The next morning when Mike got up, Uncle Joshua was nowhere to be seen. He asked his mother, "Where is Uncle Joshua? We're going to the city gallery today." He could see that his mom's eyes were ringed with red. There was a large black area on her arm. Mike could tell that she had been crying a lot. He could always tell when his dad made her cry. The marks were obvious when he hurt her. He resolved that some day when he got older, he would make his dad pay for hurting his mom. At his age, the concept of revenge for his own abuse and ill treatment had not occurred to him.

That morning she told Mike in a shaky whisper, "Your father and Joshua had a terrible fight last night. Joshua has gone home." Scaring Mike she went on, "Don't say another word. If your father hears you talking about Joshua, he will get very angry with you. I'm so sorry, I try my best to protect you from him but I can't this time. I know if he blows up again over this issue, he will hurt us both badly. Just pray with me that in time it will all pass and Joshua will be allowed back."

Mike knew from experience, what that term meant. 'Allowed back', was like when his father often in a rage would order him to his room, 'Until he was allowed back out'. It had to mean that Uncle Joshua did not leave of his own free will. For some reason he was sent away in a rage by his dad. Mike could not understand how this could happen. Uncle Joshua would never do anything bad that would cause him to be punished this way.

He thought to ask his mom what they had fought about. But when he turned to ask her, she was working at the kitchen counter, openly weeping while occasionally rubbing the black place on her arm. Mike instinctively knew, not to ask just now. It made him so sad, to know that Joshua had been sent away against his will. And once again his dad had made his mom cry, and worst of all, he had hurt her arm.

6

One month after the incident that sent Joshua away, Mike's mom got a call just before supper time. It was their neighbor Jayne. She said it was an emergency and she had to come over immediately. Mike's dad was not pleased but there was little he could do about it. Supper was put on hold as the doorbell rang.

Jayne came in looking tearful and ragged. Her hair looked like she had been wringing it. In tears she told them that her mother was seriously ill. She confessed that she had been lax about visiting her mother on a more regular basis. She begged Mike's mom, "Please help me drive to mother's this weekend?" She told his dad, I'll leave meals prepared. You and Mike can eat supper each night with my husband George. He usually drives me but he is on call this weekend. They are raising massive steel beams on the new mall parking garage. I can't drive it alone; the freeways scare me." She broke down in tears and had to be consoled by Mike's mom.

Seeing no out from the situation and wanting his supper on time, Mike's dad made a decision just to get rid of her. He told

Jayne, "The two of you can go; I don't care. As far as meals are concerned, the brat can eat with George every evening. I'm certainly not feeding him. As for me, I have places to go and eat in company that I actually enjoy." Both Mike and his mom knew where that was. When not at home or out in the wilderness, his dad's favorite place to hang out was the local sports bar. There he could watch sports, eat and drink with 'Real Men'.

That Friday Mike's mom showed him where everything he would need for breakfast and lunch was kept. She begged him to be sure to eat his suppers with George and keep to his room when his dad was home. She made sure he had her cell number and told him to call her every morning after breakfast and in the evening before he went to bed. She told Mike that George also knew about their problems and if Mike had any emergencies he could go next door for safety any time, night or day.

That long weekend was a test, and it worked out well. Mike spent all of the time that his dad was around in his room with his door closed. He sat on the floor against his bed and read a lot. At one point, getting a little bored, he dared to get out his colored pencils and an art sketch pad. He again sat against his bed and kept an ear open for house sounds. Any sound of his father's footsteps or his door handle turning, he planned to whip the sketch pad under the bed and quickly pick up his story book. Thankfully, because of his father's total disinterest in what he was doing, he was left completely alone.

Two months later his mom and Jayne went to her mother's for a five day weekend. They went again every couple of months for the next few years. Each time they returned Mike noted that his mother looked so rested and happy in spite of having to do such long distant driving. It made Mike feel good inside to see his mom happy and smiling. Happy and relaxed was a state that he seldom saw his mom in.

After each trip Jayne made a point of becoming very dramatic and enthusiastically thanking Mike's dad for letting his mom help her with the driving, telling him over and over that it was because she was afraid to drive alone on major freeways. Mike secretly enjoyed these exuberant thank-you sessions. It was a rare time when his dad looked helpless and embarrassed.

24 Nino Balistreri

7

As Mike grew up, the mood never improved at home. Mike and his mom continually lived in fear of his dad's wrath. They also had to continue hiding their activities from him, for fear of violent reprisals.

Mike grew to like the weekends that his mom went away with Jayne. He just stayed away from his dad and did his own thing. Jayne's husband George was a good guy. They had lively discussions over supper each night. George was an architect. He showed Mike drawings on his special table and explained about concrete and steel structure and commercial building design. That was his specialty. At first George was a bit stiff and shy. He and Jayne didn't have children of their own. But as the visits went on, he relaxed and was able to talk to Mike as an adult. However, George could not replace the hole in Mike's heart for his lost Uncle Joshua, but he was so pleased to have an adult male to talk to, one that didn't yell, threaten, or talk down to him.

Because his dad never mellowed in his attitude about whatever had happened that night, Mike's Uncle Joshua did not ever return. For the longest while, any time that Mike would think of Joshua he would ask his mother. He so missed their weekends together.

In time Mike painfully grew to learn not to dare ask, for fear of his dad. His dad caught him asking once. This time, there was no threat of violence. Mike learned that day how heavy and painful the back of his dads hand felt. His mother had to call the school and tell them that Mike had a bad chest infection, so would be off for a week or so. She arranged to pick up school work from his teacher so that he would not fall behind. He hated missing school, but a horribly swollen face and blackened eyes, would have been difficult to explain. It was almost two weeks before his face was clear enough to chance being seen in public.

The day after his dad had beaten him, Mike overheard his mom's friend Jayne trying to encourage her to report his father's behavior to the police. She was so shocked. When she saw the state of Mike's swollen and blackened face, she started to cry. That was the first time in Mike's life that he had indication of how wrong his father's actions were. The idea that it was illegal and could be a police matter made it so real.

Listening through his bedroom door, he heard his mom tell Jayne, "I can't. I would fear for our lives if I went to the authorities. He thinks he is a pillar of the community. He would not stand any threat to his imagined status. Especially not one coming from me. I have no access to funds of my own. He even controls my inheritance from my father. It's all I can do to beg a few dollars from it to get

Mike a few extra things for his birthday and Christmas. I have no option but to do the best that I can to protect Mike from his violence."

28 Nino Balistreri

8

Mike's dad was an engineer who operated his own small office. He made it clear from day one that his expectation was that Mike would follow in his career in order to join his firm. It wasn't because he wanted the pride of having his son work at his side. It was just a continuation of him wanting to maintain control of Mike's life and finances. To this end, his dad totally funded Mike's schooling and eventually his entry into university. He always reminded Mike that he would start off in the firm at a greatly reduced rate, until he offset his entire education and college costs.

Mike had no one to sound this against. He assumed that all parents required repayment for their child's education. The concept of having a father that loved and supported a son or daughter both emotionally and financially, was totally foreign to him.

When Mike turned twelve on April 15th, rather than giving his son a birthday present, his dad made an announcement. He told Mike, "You are old enough now to start earning your keep. I have discontinued the landscaping company. I see no point in wasting money on mowing lawns when you are here eating my food and doing nothing for it. Starting today you will be in charge of mowing and weeding. Your mother will coach you in how to weed the flower beds. And this coming winter I will not pay to have the driveway and walks cleared. You can shovel before and after school. I will expect a good job done."

Mike actually enjoyed mowing the lawns, but he hated shoveling snow. He would have done both tasks willingly and happily if he was asked to do them out of love. As he grew, for his mother's sake, he would gladly accept more responsibility to help out around the house. It just hurt that it was not about growing up, or the love of helping out. It was as always about money in his dad's pocket and his little worth as a son.

That first winter was difficult. It snowed a lot and Mike struggled to cope with the task. At first he suffered a great deal from muscle pain. But as the winter progressed he gained in muscle strength. The exertion actually helped bring on a taller and leaner growth spurt. By the time he finished high School Mike was in excellent shape. He appreciated this development, but at the same time, was sad that it had been forced on him just so his dad could pocket more money at his expense.

When he graduated high school, his Mom, George and Jayne attended the ceremony. His father refused because it meant wasting time during work hours. He only needed to know that Mike was graduating with high enough marks and had been accepted to the college program that he wanted him in.

Unknown to Mike, there was one other special person at his graduation ceremony. His Uncle Joshua sat in a back row so as not to be seen. When Mike walked up to accept his diploma, people seating next to Joshua observed him sobbing as the tears of joy ran from his eyes. They assumed that he was there for a grandchild or other family member. As soon as Mike sat back down with his class, Joshua quietly slipped from the auditorium.

That night there was a gala dance for the graduating students. Mike's mother offered to find the money if he wanted to rent a tux and take a date. She assured him that Jayne would gladly let Mike get into and out of his tux at her house, so that his dad would not know she spent the money. Mike refused his mom. First of all, there was no girl that he wanted to date. But mostly it was because he knew that his mother would have to do without and sneak the funds. The danger was too great that his dad would find out from others in the community that Mike attended the graduation ball. It would bring his wrath down on the both of them for wasting money.

Mike was anxious to start college, not because he was looking forward to his courses. He had little or no interest in engineering. He was instead looking forward to being away from the daily stress and danger of living under his father's roof. The occasional weekend home only cemented his belief that he had grown up in a toxic environment.

For the summer leading up to his first college semester, he found a job working long hours, bussing tables at a dine-in and take-out seafood cafe near home. His plan was to earn some money of his own. At the same time it would keep him away from exposure to his dad and his outdoor activities. Even this plan didn't work out. His father demanded to know how much Mike earned every week and insisted that it be split three ways. One portion he took towards

Mike's education and one portion went to his mom for the food he consumed. His mom tried to make him take her portion of the money back when his dad was not around, but Mike insisted she keep it and make a show of buying an extra fine roast or other meat or seafood item for their Sunday dinner. He knew that this would make his cheap dad happy to eat a special meal that he didn't have to pay for.

Unfortunately, for the first time in many years, there was no time in his summer routine for art. But at least his bussing tables job was keeping him well away from his dad on evenings and weekends. He was popular with the other waiting staff because he opted to not work days and took every evening and weekend shift that was available. This limited his exposure to his dad. The one thing that Michael did keep up that summer was his daily swim sessions in Jayne's pool.

Mike did well as a bus-boy. He was asked back to work the summer after his first year if college. His boss was pleased with his reliability and assured Mike that next summer he would learn to be a waiter and would earn tips if he did a good job. He gladly accepted the promise of the waiter job for the following summer. He was safe so far. He had yet to gain skills that were good enough to be of use in his dad's office. Mike knew that once he was forced to work the summers for his dad, he would see little money or recognition for his efforts.

9

That first full summer leading up to his second year, although stressful at times, went by with minimal flareups on the father side. Mike and his mom enjoyed an entire two week period alone together. His dad for the first time flew up to the Arctic for a guided fishing holiday with some of his 'Real men' friends. It was like living in another life to get up every morning and spend the entire day without tension or fear.

As September neared, Mike left home to settle into his dorm on time for the first week of classes. Mike was now in second year engineering at New Hampshire State College. He was doing well, but totally miserable studying in this field. He hated engineering. Mike found the math part of the course easy. Math came naturally to him. It was engineering that left him cold. Neither the mechanical or architectural aspect held any interest for him. But for fear of having his father enraged by a poor grade, he did his best to perform as he was expected. Other than academics, he had taken to partying with his college classmates on the weekends. He continually spurned all advances from coeds, telling them that he had a girlfriend off campus.

By near midnight on Fridays and Saturdays, Mike would always leave his college gang's gathering. If asked where he was going, he told his friends that he had a late date. Or, on occasion, for variety, he told them that his girlfriend got off work at midnight. In true fact, every Friday and Saturday night once Mike was drunk enough to get up the nerve, he would head towards downtown to the nearest gay bar.

Mike was tall handsome and fit. He was slim waist-ed but solidly built, not overly muscular. He had inherited his dad's height of six-two. He had his mother's straight sandy colored hair. From fear, combined with lack of interest, he avoided all sports participation. He had a fear of being caught looking at ass in the locker room. Or worse still, of getting an erection in the showers. The one thing that kept Mike fit was his love of swimming. He had developed this over the summers growing up. The hours spent in Jayne's pool covering up his actual summer art activities, had paid off.

He swam laps at least four times a week at the college rec center. The swim coach on several occasions tried to convince Mike to join his team. He assured Mike that he would fit in and do well with the other athletes. Mike always refused. He knew that the team horsed around in the shower room. He had witnessed it many times. Any guy play like that would have instantly boned him up.

Having a generous endowment also would cause Mike problems and embarrassment in the pool. It was easy to wear tight briefs, under loose fitting pool pants. Hiding his more than average manhood would have been impossible in a thin nylon Speedo, especially when it became erect.

When it came to Friday and Saturday nights, he was well known at the local bar. The older men knew that Mike had to be fairly drunk before he arrived. The younger ones who had the hots for Mike knew that no matter how they approached him, they had no chance.

It only took buying Mike a few more beer to make him available to any fifty-plus top who would enjoy making use of him. It was evident to everyone at the bar, Mike had severe emotional hang-ups. They naturally thought that Mike had a 'Daddy Complex'. In fact, he did, but it was not a daddy love and sex fixation, it was an obedient daddy-slave fixation that was fueled by his need to be held tight. The older clientele could easily ignore the fact that Mike had issues, especially, when springing for four or five cheap beers bought them such a hot looking and totally passive boy to enjoy.

Mike went obediently with any of the older men who chose him and plied him with the drinks that he could not afford. He submitted and obediently performed as he was instructed by them. It was just a continuation of how he had always obeyed and performed for his father. He displayed no will or enthusiasm of his own in the bedroom. Some men liked this. But many found him too passive and unresponsive to be pleasurable. But all the same, he was a fine looking young man, not to be discounted as a weekend night's entertainment.

There were men who used Mike, who claimed that he, "Came alive and responded wildly to my ardor." They were all lying to bolster their images. To everyone's disappointment, Mike had never once responded passionately to any of the daddy type's efforts.

Mike sometimes saw guys his age at the bar and at university that excited him. But he was unable to do anything about it. To make a move towards even one of them would be to him, tantamount to taking charge of his life and emotions.

Mike was fully aware of his situation. He knew where he stood mentally and emotionally. He could not be the aggressor or the instigator in any way. It would risk having the subconscious urge to take charge of other aspects of his life. Even at his young adult age, he still lived in fear of his father's wrath. Any feelings of independence or revolt were destroyed, by knowing that, like his mother, he totally depended on his dad for financial support. He had tried several times to qualify for any form of independent grants or bursaries. Unfortunately his dad was too well off financially, for Mike to qualify for these, or to get student loans that he could administer himself.

It had not been that long, since the last time his dad had blown up at him. He knew that to infuriate his dad, then return to university, was not safe. It would subject his mom to dealing with the continued rage. His mom had suffered enough over the years, doing her best to cover for Mike. She continually shielded him from his dad's violence. Sadly, she did this protecting of the son she so loved, at the constant risk of her own physical safety.

On that occasion, Mike had simply asked for a very small raise in his living allowance. Everything was extremely expensive in the university part of the city. Mike's dad threw such a rage, he actually took a swing at him. Expecting that he might do this, Mike was prepared and ducked in time. He only suffered a glancing blow, avoiding serious injury. He well knew from early childhood that bruises healed fast as long as no skin had been broken. He returned to the city the following morning vowing to get a part time job if needed, rather than ever again ask his dad for additional financial help.

After that episode, Mike planned to only occasionally go home, mostly for holidays. But even then, it was just to please his mother. He felt guilty not being there constantly, to help buffer her from his dad. But he could not be in two places at once. He actually wondered if it was easier for her when he was not at home? Not being there physically in his dad's presence, gave his dad one less issue to be upset about.

He had to concentrate on his studies. Whenever Mike was home for a weekend, he had little to say to his dad. The feeling was mutual. The only words that his dad had for Mike on the weekends were to constantly complain about his spending and expenses at school. He even made Mike replace the gas that he used driving his mom's van when he was home.

Mike's whole existence was totally open and always under close scrutiny by his dad. Every bank statement and bill was directed to his dad. Mike was unable to spend a penny for pleasure, or take part in any social activities that would involve the outlay of finances. If he did, his dad was immediately informed by his constant scanning of Mike's bank account online.

38 Nino Balistreri

10

Shortly after the violent episode over his living allowance, Mike noticed an ad in the college paper. The adjoining art college was offering an evening course in life form, one night a week. It was open to students and the public. Mike checked into the course. He found that one of the top professors from the art college was supervising the program.

At first, Mike decided that he could not afford either the time or the cost. There was certainly no way that he could ask his dad for the funds. He also knew that if he asked his mom, she would risk everything to try and sneak him the money from her already too tight household budget. He could not put his mom in that danger just so he could take an art course. It was bad enough that she risked so much over his summer art camp when he was younger. But Mike was intrigued. It was an advanced level portrait and life form course. Inquiring about possible discounts for students already enrolled at the college, he was told that the higher cost was due to the salary paid to models.

Mulling this over, Mike came up with an idea. He approached the professor in charge. It was easily arranged. Mike would be enrolled in the course. His tuition cost and purchase of supplies would be more than offset by him being added to the roster of the art college's models. Each model hired rotated through the daytime and evening classes. The Professor was delighted when Mike disrobed and modeled what he had to offer. He faithfully promised to work around Mike's daytime class schedule.

Posing nude for an art class did not bother Mike. It got a little embarrassing when he could not control his reaction to some stressful poses. Thankfully he never became fully aroused. A partial erection only enhanced his angular beauty. The professor assured Mike, after the first class in which he became semi aroused, "Mike, you are young and healthy. It is only natural that you become aroused for nothing more than a change of air currents or positioning. It happens all the time in this situation. I'm not a prude, nor is any life form artist. We take aroused body parts along with badly sagging flesh in our stride. This is truly what 'Life form' is."

Mike felt better after this talk. He actually became aroused less often after that day. It was probably due to no longer worrying about it happening. He was a natural model and soon learned all of the stock poses required in a session. As well as the nude sessions, Mike enjoyed the times that he got to pose in classic Roman Centurion armor and Greek boy togas. It fit into his passive controlled psyche, to be naked in front of strangers and told how to move about. This activity was not unlike his interaction with the older gay men on the weekends. They used and commanded him to satisfy their needs. They all believed that he had no emotional reaction to their sexual play. In a way he didn't, but he did revel in the aspect of being held tight to another human being. It was not the loving nurturing holding that he so craved and needed, but it was at least the closest to it that he had ever experienced.

On his next visit home, Mike did tell his mother about the posing job. At first she was upset. She offered to sneak money from her house account, if he needed it. But he convinced her that it was not bad. He enjoyed being part of the arts scene. He told her, "Don't worry, Mom. I am not doing anything sleazy. This is paid for by the college and completely respectable. The benefit of this job goes well beyond the excellent pay that they give me. I'm learning a lot of new techniques in my own art classes. The professor in charge is incredibly knowledgeable and completely professional."

He assured his mom, "Participating in an activity at the art college, is a part of me that I have been missing for the past few years. It's impossible for me to have a summer job and take part in art classes. Once I pay my tuition and supplies cost I actually end up with a few dollars that I can use to hang around and go out with my friends. It's money that dad can't control." His mom certainly could appreciate this fact. There could never be a penny spent for any hobbies or activities that fell within her personal interests.

Everything ran smoothly for a while. Mike enjoyed his art classes and did his stints modeling. The professor of art kept his word. He was extremely flexible, making sure that Mike's modeling sessions did not interfere with his academic schedule.

42 Nino Balistreri

11

In mid January that year Mike was doing his usual evening stint modeling for the adult life form class. That evening he could see to the back of the room where his professor was chatting with an older man. After chatting a while they walked around together viewing everyone's work. At each easel they talked with the artist. Mike wondered who the man was.

When it was time for a break, Mike donned the cotton robe that was provided for models and headed for the water fountain. As he passed his professor, he was asked to stop. He was introduced to the visitor. As soon as he heard the name, Mike knew who it was. While not being able to visit galleries for several years, he had kept up with the scene by reading the arts section of the Boston paper. It was easy to access that section. His dad always immediately discarded it as soon as he gathered the paper from the kitchen counter on his way to his den. This man was a well known Boston artist who showed at major galleries.

At the end of the class, Mike's professor asked if they could chat with him once he was dressed. The artist known simply as Mac B told Mike that he was an excellent model. He asked Mike if he would consider posing in his studio. Mike was unsure and looked to his professor. His professor assured him, "I have known Mac B for many years. He is well known and legit. I have sent him several models over the years. You need not worry; he is not a dirty old man who preys on handsome young boys like you."

With this assurance Mike told the artist, "I do need extra money to get by on. That is why I am modeling here. If it doesn't interfere with my studies, I would be pleased to pose for you.

Mac B assured Mike that he could name the time. He told Mike, "I also have a busy schedule. In the next three weeks when you can set aside a weekend, say a Friday afternoon to Sunday evening we can work together. I have a condo on Boston Harbor; there is lots of room. You will have your own room."

Mike was again not sure, knowing it would mean sleeping over. His professor spoke up right away. "Mike, you need not worry. Mac B is respectable and safe. I am a regular at his home. He will offer you excellent food and top pay. And as he does with every student that he has painted, he will give you a ride back to the university any time day or night if you should feel uncomfortable in his home."

Trusting his professor, Mike agreed to two weekends from then. For the upcoming weekend he had already committed to going home to his parents. He had to rush from class on Friday afternoon to catch the bus home. This time Mike didn't tell his mother about the new posing job. He felt that she had enough worry in her life.

As promised Mac B picked Mike up after class on the agreed upon Friday. Mike was amazed when he toured the two story condo. It was at the water's edge. He felt like he was on a boat. Mac B admitted that on two occasions a hurricane tide wet the lower level floors of the house. He told Mike that the house was solid concrete and designed to withstand a certain amount of water intrusion. It also had special high impact-resistant windows. He had only to move soft furniture, rugs and books upstairs when a hurricane was predicted.

That evening after a good meal, they sat in the living room with classical music playing and the interior lights off in order to view the harbor as it reflected the city's lights. Mike commented that the view was spectacular. In the course of conversation, Mike asked about galleries. He had not been to a Boston Gallery since he was ten. He mentioned gallery names and asked if they still existed.

Mac B explained that several were gone and named the new ones that are presently hot on the arts scene. He asked Mike, "How do you know the names of the old major galleries? They have been gone a while and you would have had to be very young to know them?"

Mike explained, "When I was small I often went to gallery openings with my uncle. But around when I was eleven my dad forced him to stay away. I still miss Joshua but have no idea where he even lives. I'm afraid to ask my mom for fear of causing her to be beaten again over the Joshua issue. My father is Joshua's younger brother. He is a horrible violent man."

Looking at Mac B, Mike realized that he had a shocked expression on his face. He asked him, "What is wrong? Did I say something that upset you."

Shaking his head, Mac B told Mike, "This is truly a small world. So you are the famous Michael. I knew your uncle for many years. I remember him bringing a tyke along to openings. I can't believe it is actually you! It has been a few years since I saw Joshua. He stopped coming to gallery openings almost ten years ago. He has several of my earlier works. If you ever re connect with him, please tell him I was asking about him. I would love to see him again."

This news shook Mike. He told Mac B, "Almost ten years ago was when my dad beat Joshua up and threw him out of our house. Was he so injured that he dropped out of the arts scene? On my next trip home I will try and have a private talk with mom. It's too dangerous. I would fear for her safety if I asked her over the phone. Dad half killed me when I was eleven and he caught me asking mom about Joshua. H beat me so bad, I missed two weeks school, so that no one would know what had happened to me. I can only hope that Mom would have somehow heard if Joshua was in trouble."

12

That night Mike slept soundly. It was helped by the three glasses of wine that he consumed and aided by the gentle sound of the waves breaking on the rocks below the patio. Bright and early Saturday morning, after a good breakfast, they got to work. Mac B took advantage of the light reflection off the harbor water as the sun traveled around the house. Every hour or so he re positioned himself and Mike. He was not overly demanding and gave Mike plenty of rest times.

That evening they again enjoyed a fine meal. Mac B confessed to having several downtown and waterfront high-end restaurants that delivered hot meals to his door. The meal that night was an amazing seafood linguine dish served with Italian salad and Italian beer. Mac B explained that it was from one of his favorite Italian restaurants along the waterfront that simply had 'Fried Calamari' painted on the awning valance.

Mike told Mac "If some day I am a successful artist I can't think of any finer way to live than what you have here. But I know that can never happen. Dad will see to it for sure that I never follow a career in art. It's amazing that I got to take all those summers of art classes behind his back. He would have killed mom and me if he had found out."

Later that evening, thanks to the four Italian beers he drank, Mike got up enough nerve to ask Mac B a personal question. He asked, "Mac, I am assuming that you are gay. Am I wrong?"

Mac B told him, "Yes you guessed right, I am gay."

Mike asked, "Well then, if you are gay, do you not find me attractive?"

Mac told him, "You are an amazingly attractive young man. No one would or could deny that fact. But I gave my word to you and your professor that you would be safe in my house, and I am a man of my word."

Mike was so used to having men Mac's age take advantage of him he was surprised to meet an honorable older man. He guessed Mac to be in his mid to late fifties, just the age range of the men from the bar who all made use of his body. He felt so comfortable and safe in Mac's home, he decided on an action. Later that evening after they had gone to bed, Mike tiptoed naked from his room and carefully slipped into Mac's bed.

Mac was startled awake when he realized that he was not alone in bed. He told Mike, "Did I do wrong and give you the impression that I wanted you in my bed? I promise that if I did, I must apologize. It was not my intention."

Mike assured him, "You did nothing wrong. I go to the bar and go with older men every weekend. I let them use me as they will. I have never felt an attraction to an older man. But I love to be held. You are so kind and you make me feel so safe, I decided that I would give myself to you willingly." As fast as he made this statement, Mike moved over tight to Mac's body.

Mac was shaken by this statement and by suddenly having Mike naked against his torso. He wrapped his arms around Mike and told him, "Because you are so trusting, you have made an old man happy tonight. Unfortunately because of cancer surgery three years ago, I am no longer able to physically respond or perform. But if you feel that way about trusting me, I would be overjoyed if you would sleep in my arms tonight."

Mike snuggled tight to Mac and soon fell asleep. A little while later he awoke. Feeling so warm and safe in Mac's arms he thought about his lonely life and the loss of the one man who loved and cared for him. He could not help but break into tears.

Alarmed Mac woke and tried to calm Mike. He asked, "What is wrong? Are you sorry that you came to my bed? You can go back to your room or even if you wish I will get dressed and drive you back to the university."

Mike told him as he sobbed, "No please. It's not you, or I mean it's not anything bad. I just got thinking about Uuncle Joshua and wishing that just once in my life I had known what it was like to be held and cuddled safely and lovingly in my dad's arms." Almost crying himself, Mac B held Mike tight and caressed his head and back until he stopped crying and slowly drifted off to sleep.

The posing sessions went well on Sunday. Mac had started a second painting. Half way through the day Mike asked Mac, "If you would enjoy the company, my first class tomorrow is not till after lunch. I have already done my studying, so if you like I can stay tonight and go back in the morning."

Mac told him, "Nothing would make me happier. Just remember I will expect you to be at the opening when the two paintings I started this weekend are being presented."

Mike promised that he would. After another excellent meal and an evening of enlightened art-related conversation, Mike again slept safely in Mac's arms. That week Mike assured his concerned art professor that all went well at Mac's studio that weekend. He didn't feel the need to go into details.

On his next two visits home, his dad was ever present. Mike had to keep a low profile and never had any alone time with his dad away from the house. The thought was too dangerous and traumatic for Mike to chance talking to his mom about Joshua. He knew that this time he would be severely beaten, not just smacked around the head like when he was eleven.

13

During the weeks that followed, Mike spent two more weekends posing for Mac B. He was pleased to finally have more money of his own. As soon as he had accumulated enough cash, he bought himself a high end tablet and a small high-quality Blue-Tooth sound system. He had always wanted these but could not dare ask for them. Nor could he ever let it be known at home that he owned such luxury items.

Three weeks before Spring break that year, Mike received an email from his dad. He was amazed! His dad had never made an effort to communicate directly with him. He always forwarded any messages or more often demands, through his mother. Politely asking his son or his wife to do anything was not part of his nature. He always communicated his wishes by authoritative commanding.

The Email was short and curt. His Uncle Joshua had died and left Mike something in his will. His dad expressed hope that it was cash, which will be applied to his education costs. It was always about money with him. He wrote to Mike that he had been approached for his college address. He informed him that an envelope was on its way from the lawyers via Courrier.

His instructions were simple, 'Sign the papers and forward them back to the lawyers, address enclosed'. His dad wrote, 'If it's not cash, it's probably useless art'. It was like a slap to Mike's psyche to have his father call it, "Useless art". Whatever it is will be sold. It will be applied to your fast-growing education debt'.

It was as always, a demand, "Will be sold and will be applied". In other words his dad planned to take it all back, to help offset his expenditures for his unworthy son's educational costs.

Thanks to his long suffering, Mike knew his dad all too well. He was not to be believed or trusted when it came to money. Every dollar spent by him or his mother had to be accounted for. Mike even had to hide the cost of the cheap beer that he took to his classmate's parties. He absorbed this into his supplies and transportation budget. It was easier to just lie about not being hungry and eat little or nothing when out with his friends. He had a cafeteria plan attached to his dorm room. Mike made sure that he ate as much as possible there. Other than that, he saved by walking or hitching rides with friends, rather than taking city transportation.

Cutting corners was safer than having his dad rage over money spent on social activities and beer. Mike knew all too well how his dad's hatred and greed worked. There was definitely something fishy going on. He had no doubt in his mind. His dad was scheming behind his back. Mike wondered, 'Does dad know what Joshua left me? Or is he assuming and wants me not to be aware'? His dad was so predictable that it was easy to read between the lines of his curt message. The unwritten message was totally clear in

Mike's mind, "I intend to steal and pocket whatever Joshua left you."

Mike's first reaction was to call his mother. Then he thought better of it. She had enough on her plate dealing with his dad. He had learned, over the years, to not put his mom in difficult positions, certainly not any that would endanger her either mentally or physically, at the hands of his dad. It had happened all too often.

Three days later, the paperwork arrived. Looking the form over, there was absolutely no indication as to what the inheritance would be. It was simply a dry legal document authorizing the law firm to act as trustees, in liquidating Mike's portion of Joshua's estate.

Mikes heart wrenched at the thought. "Liquidating the estate" had no relevance to how he felt about his loving uncle. If Joshua loved him enough to leave him something, Mike knew that it came from Joshua's heart. He was such a special person in Mike's life. He just knew that Uncle Joshua would have a more intimate message for him, in his will. The cold legal term totally smacked of his dads influence. 'Liquidating' his portion of the estate' meant nothing more than money in his dad's pocket. There would not be a penny's grace for him or his mom.

14

For the first time in his life, Mike became furious. It was his inheritance, not his dad's. He was livid thinking, 'That bastard never let me see Uncle Joshua again. He didn't even have the decency to tell me why. The argument that awful night and Uncle Joshua being thrown out of our house has to be Dad's fault; I know him too well. Mom loved Uncle Joshua as much as I did. She would never treat him that way. It is obvious that dad's hate caused Joshua to be thrown out. Neither mom nor Joshua would ever do this to me. I can admit it now! After Joshua left for good, I never truly felt happy at home. There was nothing to look forward to. It's just not right. No mother or child should live in fear, afraid to ask an honest question because they might get beat upon'.

That day Mike made a groundbreaking decision for the first time, totally on his own and with no fear of reprisals. The following day he called Mac B. He asked if he could come over either for the weekend or just for overnight on Sunday. He told Mac. "I am so sad, Uncle Joshua has died. I got a letter from a lawyer that was directed by my hateful father. He wants me to sign over for liquidation, whatever Joshua left me. I have no idea what that is, but I know for sure that my father is planning to put it all in his own pocket. I will never see a penny."

Mac told mike, "I am also saddened that Joshua is gone. It would have been wonderful to see him again and remember old times together. I have commitments for Friday evening and an association brunch to attend Saturday morning. I will call you as soon as I am free Saturday and come pick you up."

True to his word, Mac called Mike early Saturday afternoon. Mike was so pleased to be able to spend time with him. He needed someone to talk to about Joshua, someone who knew Joshua and would not beat him for talking. It saddened him that he could not go home for the weekend and talk to his mother.

Knowing why Mike was coming over, Mac had searched in his archives and was able to locate slides that he had taken of the three pieces that Joshua bought. He explained to Mike, "Back in the day we didn't have computers. We took slides of all our work as they were hung for showing. I am an old fashioned guy. I continued to take slides a long while after everyone switched to digital photography and computers. In the end though, I had to break down and open my mind to the new technology. You are fortunate in that you grew up with computers. You didn't have to experience all the hair pulling and screaming at the screen in order to learn." They both had a good laugh over that statement.

Before leaving the condo Sunday evening, he thanked Mac for the support and for the offer to accompany him to the lawyers and later a drive back to the dorm. He told Mac, "If I am finally going to take control of my life, it has to start now."

Spending the time with Mac and talking about Joshua helped calm Mike and cement his resolve in what he needed to accomplish. The following morning he skipped his Ethics lecture and took the commuter train into downtown Boston. Going straight to the law firm, Mike showed the receptionist the legal papers. He asked, "I would like to speak to the lawyer who sent me this information."

She objected, stating, "We do not allow drop-ins. If you wish to seek legal representation, you must call in advance for an appointment."

Mike told the receptionist, "I'm in college at New Hampshire State. I took today off and the train to town, because I need to sign these papers. I am just not sure about a few things. I need to ask the lawyer a couple of questions before I sign. I can't take another day off. We are nearing finals."

Reluctantly, she picked up the in-house phone and called the lawyer. Mike was shortly ushered into a lavish office. His only thought was, 'Law obviously pays better than engineering. Dad's offices are shabby compared to these. Or then again, what do I know? Engineering might also be lucrative and dad's office is shabby because he is so cheap.

The lawyer introduced himself as Walter Perkins. He obviously had better things to do, so tried to rush Mike along. He spread out the papers, made check marks on spaces with a yellow highlighter and then handed Mike a pen to sign with.

Mike set the pen down and stated, "I won't sign until I know what I've inherited. These papers tell me nothing."

In response Mr. Perkins told him, "Your father has given us clear instructions. It's all arranged. Just sign and we will take care of everything for you and your dad."

That was all that Mike needed to hear. Something deep inside him snapped. For the first time in his life, the long building rage in his being gave him the strength to take complete charge of a situation. Looking the lawyer in the eye, he all but screamed, "I am of age as of this month. From now on you deal with me. If you choose to have any further contact with my father, I promise I will report you to the bar. I am your client, not my father. He no longer has legal power over me."

Shocked, Mr. Perkins apologized, "I am sorry Mr. Nicholas. I assumed that you were in total agreement with your father over this issue. That was certainly the impression he gave me, when he laid out his instructions for liquidating your uncle's estate. If this is not the case, again I apologize. What can I do for you to make the process easier?"

Mike asked, "Did you tell my dad what I inherited or what it was worth?"

Mr. Perkins replied, "No, your dad did not ask. When I told him the reason for trying to contact you, he faxed me a letter with instructions. It was very precise and clear. Actually I have it here in your file."

Handing the fax to Mike, he read what his father had demanded.

"I will allow you to contact my son strictly in order to get his signature. I want to make it clear. Anything that is left to him, other than cash, is to be liquidated. My son does not wish to have anything that belonged to his uncle. Our family did not get along with Joshua. As far as we are concerned, he was a horrible person. He had no children of his own. It's only right that he mention his only nephew in his will."

To add insult to injury, his dad had the nerve to add to his lie, "I am deeply in debt over my son's university costs. He needs cash to pay down his loans and mine."

This really did it. Mike told Mr. Perkins, "There is no debt or loans. My father is well off. He is also violent and miserably cheap. He is trying to steal my inheritance.

"My mother and I loved Uncle Joshua. He was a wonderful human being, unlike my father. It's amazing that they were actually brothers. No two humans could ever be more different."

Mike decided, "I want to read the will and know what my uncle's wishes were. Also I want to know, exactly just what I inherited."

Mike had not only shocked the lawyer, he had shocked himself. Being assertive and standing up for his rights was something that he would never have dreamed of doing, especially behind his father's back. He feared him too much.

15

That day an embryo had formed. It was the beginning of a new person, one who had power and confidence, a new man who had strength and conviction to make the decisions that would shape his own future.

In spite of his new found strength, Mike feared what the consequence of his actions would be for his mother. If he stood up to his dad, it would go badly at home. She would be the one left behind to bear the brunt of his uncontrollable and violent rage. Mike decided, 'Wherever my new found strength takes me, I will have to build in protection for Mother'. It was important to him that she should escape his father's mental and physical abuse.

Mr. Perkins called his secretary. She promptly brought in Joshua's file. He opened it up and handed a sheaf of papers to Mike. He announced, "Here it is Mr. Nicholas, your uncle's will. You can have this copy to keep." He also handed Mike a thick envelope, "There are three sets of keys and deed papers included in this envelope. Basically, he left you his entire estate. It includes his home on the Cape and its contents, as well as his savings and investments.

"He must have had a premonition well before he became ill. Nine years ago he had our tax team make changes to his financial set-up. He made you, in-trust with him, an equal owner of all that he possessed. By doing this enough years in advance, he was able to circumvent almost all of the actual inheritance taxes involved in your taking full charge of the estate.

"Personally I was not involved in that transaction but I believe that your mother was. Someone of age would have signed on your behalf. Knowing what I now know, your father was obviously not involved in that procedure. I can see by his file that we did contact Joshua two months ago with regards to your coming of age. At that point, he requested that we hold off contacting you. It was because of his health. He informed my partner that he was dying and that we would be required to shortly deal with his will and turn his estate over to you. That is why I contacted your father to gain your address. Obviously, your mother never saw that request or she would have directed us to you in an appropriate way. We only had a reply from your father."

In shock at this news, Mike opened the cover of the file. He was stunned, his head was spinning. He glanced at the contents page. It looked as if Uncle Joshua was well off and now, so was he. The implications of actually being master of his own financial life were completely staggering.

With shaking hands, he opened to the second page of the file. Attached to the first page of the formal will, there was a cover letter from Joshua. He stated; "I truly missed being part of Michael's life.

My fervent wish is that Michael is able to overcome his father's controlling grasp and make my Cape house his home."

Reading this line, Mike had the strangest reaction at seeing his name in print as 'Michael'. Pushing this thought aside, he shocked himself with another fast decision. "I have decided not to sign this paperwork today. I will wait a while and think about it. If these are the keys to Uncle Joshua's house, can I have them now? I plan to go and check things out over spring break. Once I'm clear on everything, I'll notify you if anything is to be disposed of."

Mike had a further thought. His mind was now working in hyper speed, almost beyond control. "If I decide to let everything stand as is, according to my uncle's wishes, what must I do?"

Mr. Perkins assured Mike, "If you keep everything as your uncle willed, you have only to make an appointment with me to sign off on the account. Smiling, he added, "And of course, you need to settle the account for any outstanding billing time such as today's visit."

Mike surprised himself with one more question. He had no idea where it came from, but knowing that Uncle Joshua trusted this firm, it must be a good one. He asked, "Does your firm also have lawyers who are top notch in Matrimonial law, lawyers that are good at fighting and winning heavy duty divorce settlements?"

With a surprised look, Mr. Perkins replied, "Yes. We have an extremely strong team that deals exclusively with divorce law. Our record is excellent in achieving financial security for our clients." He then asked Mike, "I thought that you were simply a student? We had no indication that you are married or we would have required your wife's signature as well."

Mike assured Mr. Perkins, "No, I am not married, but my mother is unfortunately married to my abusive father. With this security supporting me, things might need to drastically change for Mom."

Having said this much, Mike knew that he was nearing physical and mental exhaustion. His head was flying and his stomach churning. He was afraid that he would upchuck right in the lawyer's office. It was time to get out of there and chill.

Mike handed Mr. Perkins a sheet of paper, "Here is my Email for future reference. I will notify you as soon as I have a new phone number. Meanwhile, please, use my Email address if you need to contact me.

"I remind you, that I am now your client. I do not give permission for my father to have access. That includes my dealings with you, or any of this information about the scope and worth of the estate."

Mr. Perkins handed over a large envelope for Mike's copy of the will, as well as another one containing the keys and address of the house. He added, "Included in this envelope is the entry code for the alarm system, as well as a smaller envelope that contains keys for the vehicles. They are both locked in the garage."

This was staggering news, vehicles! Mike had never owned even one. He drove his mother's old van, or took transit when he was at home for weekends and school breaks. His dad had never let him near his car. He had also refused to allow Mike to have his own car.

When Mike was preparing for his first term he had broached the subject of buying a small car. His dad angrily told him, "No way,

I don't give a damn how inconvenient it is. You can take the bus, walk, crawl, or hitchhike, if necessary. I refuse to waste money on a car, just so you can joy ride around the city on my dime while entertaining your college gang."

Shaking Mr. Perkins hand and thanking him, Mike left the office. Once out of the office complex, he had to lean against the corridor wall for nearly ten minutes. His head was so wildly spinning he felt weak kneed and dizzy. He was unable to move forward. Looking around, he wished that there was a chair or bench to sit on. He had spotted benches and small coffee tables in the lobby of the building, but was sure that he would buckle at the knees before he reached them. Instead he slid to the floor and sat a while, propped up against the wall.

The shock of learning about his inheritance, added to being strong and assertive for the first time in his life, was staggering. It was just too much to handle. A few minutes later, two business suited men, carrying briefcases exited the elevator and headed for the lawyer's office. Seeing Michael sitting on the floor, they stopped and asked if he was all right. It was obvious that this young man was extremely pale and looked in distress. He assured them that he was fine and just needed to rest a bit before heading on. Several minutes later, the lawyer's receptionist came out. The men had obviously told her that there was a young man on the floor in the corridor. Recognizing Mike, she offered to call security in order to get him some medical assistance. He assured her that he was fine, and just needed a few minutes to get his head straight. She offered to bring him out a chair to sit on but he assured her that he would be OK. She told him that she would check on him again in a few minutes. Mike was able to stand, more or less steadily, and head for the elevators before she returned.

16

As Mike rode the commuter train back to the University, the rocking of the carriage and the rhythm of the wheels rolling against the tracks helped to calm him a bit. At least it helped to bring his breathing below the hyperventilation state. His heart and breathing had been racing wildly for the past few hours. All that he was able to manage was to sit still and grasp the lawyer's large envelope to his chest.

Now thinking with a head that was still spinning, but no longer totally out of control, Mike slowly started to formulate his plans. When he got back to the residence, he called Mac B. He told him, "I have just returned from the lawyer's. Joshua left me his home on the Cape and his entire estate. I have no idea what it all entails; I am too shocked to sort it right away."

Mac B offered, "If I can be of any help, don't hesitate to call me. If you need to go to the Cape, I can either drive you, or if I'm not available, I will rent you a car. Anything I can do, I will be pleased to help for both your and Joshua's sake." Mike thanked him and promised that he would call if he needed anything.

That night Mike barely slept. His mind would not rest. He tried listening to music, and then reading. Nothing would lift the burden of his new situation. In the early morning light he made a decision. The following day he called his mother. He hated to have to lie to her, but under the circumstances he had no choice. In order to protect her from his dad's wrath, this time he had to make an exception.

Thankfully she answered the phone. It would have been a great deal more awkward if his dad had picked up the receiver. He told her, "Chandler and some of my friends are going to a ski chalet in Vermont for spring break. I can ride up with them and stay in the chalet. It belongs to my classmate's dad. If Dad gives you flack, tell him not to sweat. I will not be wasting money. My transportation and room are free. Also there will be no lift fees, because as you know, I don't ski. Tell him I will use my break time up there to relax and get ahead in my studies. That will appease him.

"You can make him happy, by telling him that it will save him money. If I was home for the week it would cost more to feed me and put extra gas in your van." To help ease his mother's disappointment, he told her, "I'll miss seeing you next week, but I'll make a point of coming home within the next two weeks or so. I know that you were looking forward to me being home for spring break, but it's important that I go away. I can't explain right now, but I will later. I promise that you will understand."

That evening he told his dorm-mate Chandler, "I'm not going directly home for the break. I'm in a personal mess and have elsewhere to go for a few days in order to straighten things out. Please, if you must call me, call my cell number. Not under any circumstances are you to call my parent's number. I can't have them involved in my situation. My dad would wreck everything, plus it would put my mom in danger.

"Chandler, I really need you to help me in this. I hated to do it, but I had no choice but to lie to my mother. I told her that I was going with you and some classmates, to a chalet for the week. Please, you have to trust me. I promise, I will explain it all later, but I just can't right now."

A shocked Chandler exclaimed. "Oh My God, Mike, are you in trouble with the law? My dad has a good lawyer; he will gladly hire him to help you out. Please don't hesitate to ask. We are friends; I would do anything to help you."

Mike assured Chandler, "No, I am not in legal trouble. It's a family thing that I must sort out on my own. I can't tell you or anyone right now. I wish I could tell my mother, but she would be in physical danger if my father found out. Please don't worry about me. I have everything under control. I will tell you everything soon, but I must beg you to cooperate. Remember, only contact me on my cell phone and if my parents should by chance call you, back up my story of being at a chalet with you. Just tell them that I am out for a run or something. But if they do call, warn me so I can return the call. The only thing that I can tell you now is that it relates to my Uncle Joshua's death. But it is not a bad thing. You will understand once I am able to explain what is happening."

A totally puzzled Chandler assured Mike, "I will do as you ask. Just be safe and please be sure to call me if you need anything or are in any trouble. I will be at home all week, and as you know, I have a car at my disposal, so I can help you out on short notice."

17

In fact, the Saturday morning that spring break began, Mike left for Cape Cod. One of his classmates lived there. He hitched a ride with him, under the guise of visiting his uncle. Once clear of Boston, Mike called Mac B and left a message. "Hi Mac, it's Mike. I am on my way to the Cape. A classmate is giving me a lift. His parents live near where I am going. Everything is fine. I will call you later in the week to fill you in. Thanks again for your offer to help. I will not hesitate to take you up on it if I have a need."

The day had dawned cool and clear. Crossing over Buzzard's Bay, Mike found it hard to carry on a normal conversation with his classmate Victor, who was anxious to get home for the break. Mike found this amazing. He could never look forward to a week in his dad's home, even if it meant time with his mother. The stress involved destroyed any possible feelings of happiness. Every mile that they traveled, his nerves and excitement escalated. A couple of times he came really close to asking Victor to pull over so that he could upchuck in the ditch. He was on a journey into the unknown.

Mike believed that today was going to be the beginning of a new life, one that would nurture and develop the embryo of his new self assured personality, a milestone in his life.

Victor dropped him and his gym bag off at the foot of Joshua's driveway. Then he returned to the main road. It was twenty miles further to where his parents lived on the outskirts of Provincetown. He promised Mike that he would give him a call later in the week to let him know when he would pass by on his way back.

The entrance to the driveway was crowned by sandstone pillars that supported ornate metal gates. A tall manicured hedge acted as a privacy wall that filled in the balance of the street front. The ornate metal gates were propped open. They looked as if they had seldom if ever been closed. On the face of the left pillar, the house numbers were boldly displayed on a brass plaque that was set into the stone work. On the face of the right pillar, another brass plaque announced the name of the house. Mike stood a minute to absorb this. The house was called, 'Casa Del Mer'.

Mike slowly walked the winding cobblestone drive, taking in every detail. Along the edges of the winding drive, there was a raised curb. It held back a cedar mulched bed of flowering bushes. They were as neat as the hedge on either side of the entrance pillars.

Mike observed each one as he passed. He knew some were roses. He only really knew what he had learned from his mother, how to distinguish weeds from flowers. Never having actually gardened, he had no idea what the other flowers and bushes were called.

The condition and neatness of the surrounding grounds suggested that they were being professionally tended. Mike thought, 'Oh God, what does it cost to keep this all up? I hardly have any of my own money. I am sure that my little income from modeling would never come close to maintaining all this. There is no way that Dad will help out. If there is little actual money in the estate, I am screwed. It would be horrible to be forced to do as he demanded and have to sell the place. Joshua's wishes were that I make his home my own'.

The cobblestones on the entire driveway were covered with a fine dusting of sand. There was no sign that anyone had driven on it in a while. It wound past small sand dunes that were crowned with clumps of exotic grasses and wild roses. Every few feet along on both sides of the drive, stood short stone pillars with ornate iron lanterns mounted on each peak. Rounding the last sharp bend, Mike stopped dead in his tracks. The driveway had opened onto a large circular area that like the driveway was ornately laid in cobblestones.

The house was quite a large-sized Salt Box. It was beautiful. It had gray wood shake siding and a medium blue steel roof with matching blue shutters and white window trim.

Along the foundation rested a cedar-mulched garden. It was dotted with small green shrubberies, but no flowers. He could just see the ocean through the dunes on either side of the structure. Mike's mind was raging now, 'To think that I almost lost this, thanks to my greedy father'.

He let himself into the house with the key and punched in the alarm system deactivation code. Mike was stunned and amazed.

He could see from the spacious foyer thay the rooms were open and bright, even with the draperies drawn. As he slowly walked through the living area, he had a warm feeling that his presence was making the house come to life. The living and dining rooms were beautifully furnished and decorated. Mike thought, 'Uncle Joshua always dressed well. Did he also create all of this or was he wealthy enough to hire professionals?' Wandering from the foyer, through the living room, dining room and amazing stainless steel modern kitchen, he then worked his way down the center hallway.

In a trance-like state, Mike glanced into a small library and three bedrooms. Two of the bedrooms were spacious and grand looking. They were each as large as the master bedroom in his parents' home. Between the den and the two bedrooms there was a spacious modern bathroom. It had a small window that lit the room a bit. Mike thought at first that a light had been left on. Looking closer he realized that the circle of light beaming from the ceiling was actually a type of skylight. He had seen one of these in a classmate's parents' home. The third bedroom looked large enough to be a home in itself. Mike thought, 'Wow, I could fit at least six of the dorm bedrooms into here'.

Not entering any of these rooms, in a trance like state, Mike re-traced his steps to the rear of the living room. On his way there he had a passing thought. 'There are three dormers on the land side of the roof. But I don't see a staircase, or a visible trap door to the attic'. Leaving this thought for now, he continued to examine everything around in the living room. The furniture was elegant and very expensive looking. The walls were tastefully hung in beautiful oil paintings. Mike paused in front of each painting to take in its meaning and mood.

Finally reaching the back wall, he searched out the pull cords for the wall of draperies, but found none. Turning, he spotted what he had originally thought was a TV remote sitting on an end table. But unlike a remote this unit had only two buttons. Pressing them he was surprised as he stood in a trance and watched the entire wall of luxurious draperies glide open to the sound of an electric motor. It exposed an entire wall of glass.

Unlocking and gliding open the multi-paneled sliding doors, he walked out onto a large deck that overlooked low lying sand dunes, with the beach and rolling surf beyond. The deck was in the same state as the driveway, covered with a dusting of sand with no sign of being walked on in a while. The panoramic view was totally enrapturing. Mike slipped out of his shoes and socks, then stepped down onto the warm sand. He was drawn towards the rolling surf, but after a few steps, he stopped and turned back to the deck. He picked up his shoes and socks intending to put them back on, but he just stood on the deck mesmerized by the beautiful view of Cape Cod Bay. After a few minutes he turned around and re-entered the house. He was in such a daze that he failed to look up while on the deck, and did not notice the full width dormer that spanned the entire water side of the roof.

18

Mike finally realized, exclaiming aloud to himself, "O. M. G. I HAVE TO BE RICH! Only a millionaire lives like this."

The implications were staggering. Mike had been so caught up in classes and studying for finals the past three weeks. He had only worked on planning his escape to the Cape. He had not delved into the lawyer's bulky envelope. Mike trotted barefoot to the front of the house. He dropped his shoes and socks by the door and reached for his bag, still resting abandoned in the foyer. Drawing out the large envelope, he walked to the kitchen, sat at the kitchen table, opened the envelope and carefully drew the sheaf of legal papers out onto the table's surface. With a feeling of reverence Mike carefully leafed through the pages.

He soon spotted what he was looking for. Buried among the many pages of his uncle's official file, he found the estate's financial statement. Mike's eyes could barely be contained in their sockets. Uncle Joshua left checking and savings accounts, adding up to over two hundred and fifty thousand dollars. There was also a broker's statement, showing three hundred and seventy-five thousand dollars in blue chip stocks. It also contained a statement from a mortgage company giving the final release for a paid-in-full mortgage.

Mike sat there for over a half hour, stunned. He slowly read the entire sheaf of papers over three times, before it totally sank in. A letter attached to the financial statement gave the name and address of a nearby Cape Cod bank. It informed Mike that he would have to go in with a copy of the will and photo ID. It reminded him that he had to sign official transfer papers, before he could gain access to the checking and saving accounts. There was also a letter from the stock brokerage firm that handled Uncle Joshua's account. A trip to Boston to meet with them and sign further papers was requested.

Mike thought about this for a bit. He then formed at least an immediate plan. He would call the bank first thing Monday morning and make an appointment to get this phase done right away. That way, he would have access to immediate cash, other than his living allowance account. It would be safer for both him and his mom not to use his own account. Doing it this way would assure that there are no expenditures showing for the Cape on his own bank statement. That statement went directly to his dad every month, so that he could approve or, more often, raise hell over every penny that Mike spent. His dad had never trusted him with a credit card. He was sure that having such grand funds, the bank would waste no time in issuing him one. He was thankful at least that he had some cash in his pocket that he had earned posing for Mac B and the art college. He could survive till the bank opened on Monday.

Then Mike slowly formulated a further plan. Once he was back at college, he would go to his bank and transfer his entire school account to his mother. It would be up to her to either keep it, or give part or all of it to his dad. On second thought, he was sure that his dad would demand every penny from her. Mike decided to just transfer it back directly to his dad, as soon as he made his final trip home to deal with his new situation. This would save having his mother being humiliated and forced to hand over the lousy little bit of money that he had to survive on every month.

When that was done, he planned to close that account completely and stop dealing with his father's bank. He never wanted to be connected in any way to his father's world. Mike never wanted to see another hatefully begrudged penny from his dad. He also wanted to ensure that his dad had no connection to his new accounts or any other aspect of his new life. Right from when he was little, every dollar that was spent on Mike's behalf had always been reluctantly given, with severe conditions attached. Mike was still not clear in his head. It would take a while to totally accept that he was finally free from his dad's tyranny.

Then, another plan started to form in his head. But this plan would have to wait until he had the banking and legal issues settled. Then he could safely go ahead with it.

80 Nino Balistreri

19

Late that afternoon, while Mike was slowly exploring the cupboards and drawers in the living and kitchen areas, he received a call from Chandler, his college roommate of two years.

"Hey Mike, I'm at my parents. It's hell here. They are all fighting over the vast amounts of money that my mother and sister are throwing around. It is all for sis's upcoming June wedding.

"My God Mike, you would think we were royalty the way they are planning and spending. Dad is in a state over it all. Amazingly, he is not blaming Mom. He says that she has been brainwashed by the lavish weddings on the soaps and that Hallmark channel. I swear, he is wavering between breaking down in tears and having a major stroke, every time they announce a further major expenditure."

Mike sympathized with him, "That's too bad, Chandler. But knowing your mother and sister, I am not surprised that they got carried away. Last month when we were at your place for the long weekend, I couldn't help but overhear some of the wild ideas that they were cooking up. Both your sis and mom had a strange surrealistic look on their face, while talking about the wedding plans.

"Your dad has never been strong at standing up to your mom. He is so kind, a much too gentle man to put his foot down and rein in the expenditures. He could certainly take lessons from my bastard dad. But then he would no longer be the great guy that he is. You have no idea how fortunate you are in having him for a dad."

Shocked at this statement, Chandler asked, "Why, what happened? Are you in trouble? Aren't you home now? Is that why you didn't want me to call you there?" Chandler added, "I know that I lucked out with both my parents. They are everything that a son could wish for in spite of my sis and Mom's grandiose wedding fantasies."

Mike confessed, "I'm sorry, I didn't tell you the real truth about this week, but I had to check out things for myself. I did tell you that my uncle Joshua died and left me something in his will. Well, he left me his house on the Cape. I am here now. My bastard dad tried to swindle me out of it. Thankfully, I smartened up at the very last minute, or I would have lost it all. I almost didn't get the nerve to go through with it; I am so used to living in fear of that bastard. But I met an old friend of my uncle's who gave me the strength of will to face it all and short circuit my greedy dad."

Chandler exclaimed, "Wow that is amazing! Your own house! Do you need help for the week? I'm desperate to get the hell out of this madhouse, before I get sucked into their high finance vortex. Both sides are trying to get my support, like it has anything to do with me. If I dare to open my mouth with even a small opinion,

I will be immediately in a no-win situation. She might be my sister, but I am not her guardian. The money issue over her wedding is between her and my parents."

Chandler added, "I have my own allowance from the education plan that Mom and Dad bought when I was born. As you know, it's bolstered monthly by a small endowment, from my grandfather's estate. I'm not rich, but as long as I'm careful, I manage quite well on it. So far the only real mad money cash that I get on a regular basis from Mom and Dad, is on the sly. Having said that, don't get me wrong, I'm not broke. I learned from my granddad to keep a nest egg for emergencies and special occasions. If you are in trouble Mike, just say the word and all that I can scrape up is yours."

Surprised at this statement about secret cash from Chandlers parents Mike asked, "Why on the sly? Are they in disagreement? I can certainly understand how that works. Do they actually have to slip you cash behind each other's back? My father would never give me a penny of cash and when my mother tries to, I always refuse it well knowing that she is going behind Dad's back to short her grocery and household budget in order to offer it to me."

Chandler laughed, "No, you have that totally wrong. It's nothing like your situation. It's like a game they play. Don't ask me why, but it really is cute. Possibly it's what their parents did when they were in university who the hell knows? But every time I am home, at one point when no one is looking, Dad tucks a few twenties into my pocket and winks. He then whispers to me, "Use this to have some fun". He often adds "All work and no play makes Chandler a dull boy. Then for certain, every weekend home, Mom does the same. But being the practical one she whispers, "In case you need some new clothes or supplies. I like it when you are smartly dressed.

"That is the funniest part of this current mess. Mom has always been the practical half of their marriage. She continually reminds Dad about budgets, when he gets carried away with a wildly expensive idea. What is happening to her personality over this extravagant wedding fiasco is truly amazing. It has no basis in Mom's normal psyche."

Chandler went on, "Mike, you have to help me now. I will gladly bring my check book to bail you out. But in return, please save my ass. Let me come to the Cape to give you a hand. My sanity is at stake if I stay here for the entire week!"

Mike had always loved every minute that he spent with his roommate. Their evenings together studying and listening to music were his favorite. They had become comfortable around each other, early in their first year of rooming together. Standard dress in their shared dorm room had always been boxers or briefs. When he was dressing, Mike always attempted to engage Chandler in conversation at just the right moment. It always caused Chandler to face him naked to reply.

Responding to Chandler's plea, Mike jumped at the opportunity. "Yes, please come, I am all but overwhelmed. It will be great to have help and company." Mike didn't say a word about the money issue. Thinking, 'Chandler will find out that there is no need for financial help quickly, as soon as he arrives at the Cape house'. He gave Chandler the address and directions for the Cape house. He knew that Chandler had his own car. Immediate transport to the Cape would not be a problem.

Mike was anxious now. He was feeling so strong and in control. He was afraid of how he would now handle being close to Chandler and not make a fool of himself. He feared ruining their friendship by making an overt sexual advance towards him. He thought, 'I will be careful to not drink too many beers while Chandler is here. If I stay sober, I will have better control and be able to resist making a pass at him'.

86 Nino Balistreri

20

Ending the call, Mike had a sudden revelation. 'Oh God, cars! I'm in such shock over the house and estate. I forgot to look in the smaller envelope of extra paper work, or go into the garage to see what is in there'.

On the far side of the kitchen, there was a side door. Mike walked from the living room and through the kitchen. He opened the side door and peered into complete darkness. There were no windows opening from the garage to the outside. Nothing could be seen in the blackness. He felt the inside wall beside the door and found a switch. Flipping it on, Mike stood on the door sill, frozen, unable to step forward. Now illuminated by ceiling lighting, two vehicles came into focus. One was a beautiful white Mazda hard top, two seat sports car. Parked beside it, sat a really cool tan colored Sahara Jeep. It had a canvas top, with large overhead lights attached to a roll bar.

It seemed to take forever before Mike was able to step forward and actually touch the vehicles, to assure his addled mind that they were for real. They were so beautiful. He was afraid that they might be a fantasy conjured from his imagination.

Once he walked completely around both vehicles, taking in every inch of their amazing shapes, Mike got up enough nerve to try and open the driver's door on the Jeep. Finding it locked, he remembered that the envelope in the kitchen contained sets of keys. He quickly returned to the kitchen and retrieved the keys from the lawyers' envelope. Having gone this far, he got up enough nerve to unlock both vehicles and sit behind the wheels. It was a good thing that no one was nearby. Mike was in a stunned state.

When he finally climbed out of the second vehicle, he wandered around the garage. The interior of the garage was completely finished as if it was the house interior. It had a shiny blue Spackle floor coating and pastel painted walls. Like the entire house, it was spotless. There was heavy duty steel shelving, for storage along the far outside sidewall. The shelves were mostly empty except for the top of each unit. These shelves were filled with large plastic bins that were all labeled 'Christmas interior' or 'Christmas exterior'.

The back wall of the garage had a custom-designed metal workshop cabinet system and work bench that spanned the entire width. The work bench was clear and spotless. It looked like it had never been used for its designed purpose. On the opposite wall nearest the house, hung a few basic garden tools, and a heavy duty push broom, and an electric blower for clearing the sand off the deck and driveway. There were also several folding beach chairs and floats neatly hung in a row. The lack of any real garden care equipment cemented the fact in Mike's mind that the grounds were definitely being professionally groomed.

Once back in the house, Mike had to sit a while, attempting to grasp it all and clear his head. He suddenly realized that he was ravenously hungry. Looking in the double-door fridge he could only see pickles, jam and a few basic condiments. Thankfully, there was a six pack of beer. He wondered if Uncle Joshua drank this, or if he left it behind hoping that Mike would find it. He found a frozen pizza and little else in the large bottom drawer freezer. This would do just fine for tonight. Mike decided that first thing tomorrow, he would take the Jeep and find the local grocery store. Now that Chandler was coming, they needed food and definitely more beer.

While the pizza was cooking in the upper of the two wall ovens, Mike went to the hall cupboard. It was a large floor to ceiling antique-looking wardrobe. Although it seemed like an actual free standing piece of furniture, Mike had the sensation that it was more than snugly attached to the house itself. He thought, 'It's probably mounted that way to be safe. That would prevent it from tipping when it's heavily loaded'.

Opening the large door he selected sheets and pillowcases from the shelf marked master bedroom. He noted that another shelf was for sheets for the guest bedrooms. He wondered if it was always this way or if his uncle labeled them to make it easier for him to figure it out? The upper two shelves contained bedspreads and comforters. One lower shelf was filled with expensive looking matched sets of towels. The bottom shelf was bursting full of colorful beach towels.

Entering the master bedroom for the first time, Mike was startled at the sight. Uncle Joshua was ever so kind and thoughtful. The king size bed was topped with a beautiful thick new mattress, still clad in its manufacturer's vinyl wrapper.

It was evident that Joshua wanted to make sure that Mike would not have to sleep in the bed that he either died or was ill in. As he set the bedding down, he glanced at the side table nearest him, He recognized the two devices that were sitting there. One was a remote for the TV and the other was the same as the living room, a remote to operate the draperies. He hit the button and watched in awe as the draperies slid open to reveal another wall of glass overlooking the large deck, and beyond, an amazing view of the sand dunes and ocean.

He next wandered into the adjoining master bath. It was nothing short of amazing, just like in a magazine. It had double vessel sinks that rested on an almost wispy veined white-marble counter and a large glass walled walk-in shower. There was also a free-standing, deep, soaking tub. It looked big enough for at least two adults. The floor and walls of the entire room was finished in the most beautiful white butterscotch-veined marble.

Michael had seen marble exactly like this before. But it was certainly not in his home. His dad was too cheap to spring for any luxury finishing s. He had experienced it in a university friend's home. His friend's parents had proudly displayed their master bathroom floor covered in this Italian Carrera marble. It was a personal souvenir, to remember their second honeymoon trip to Italy.

Staring at the marble, Mike thought, 'A second honeymoon trip. Amazing! My hateful dad even balked at a free weekend on the Cape because it would have meant taking "Family" time. I would have been so happy to spend time with Joshua in his home rather than trying to enjoy his visit to our house while avoiding criticism and interference from Dad. He peeked into the large walk-in closet. It was extremely neat, but filled with clothes. Seeing these brought back a childhood memory. Uncle Joshua was always smartly dressed when he took Mike out and about on weekends. He wore extra smart clothes when they went to the gallery openings.

This gave him an idea. He planned to call Mac B. It was hard to remember after all these years, but the clothes looked like they might fit Mac. He planned to have Mac visit and choose what he wanted before Mike donated it all to charity. It all looked expensive. Mike took a pair of pants from a hanger and held them up to himself. They were too small in the waist and at least four inches too short. When he was ten he not only saw Uncle Joshua as being an amazing and brilliant person, he also believed him to be very tall. Obviously, Joshua was shorter than both he and his dad. It was his importance in Mike's life that elevated him to great heights of stature in his mind.

He thought, 'Chandler will be able to help me deal with all this'. Mike was so happy that his roommate was coming. After a beer and three slices of pizza, he removed the mattress wrapping and made up his bed. He decided to set up the guest room for Chandler in the morning.

On the way back to the kitchen, Mike stepped into the den for the first time. He switched on the light and looked around. There was no desk or filing cabinet as he had expected. Instead it was set up with two overstuffed easy chairs, and a wall of custom cabinets and shelving. Looking closer Mike found an amazing sound system, including a turntable. The glass door cabinets revealed collections of novels and collectibles, as well as hundreds of LP records.

As he turned to leave his eyes rested on the back wall behind the sofa chairs. He recognized the art right away. The three pieces of Mac B's art looked amazing in this elegant setting. They were all modern abstract interpretations of historic structures. Each had a small brass plaque on the frame that announced the scene, one each of Rome, Paris and Casablanca. Mike thought, 'Joshua must have traveled a lot. I so wish I could have listened to his tales of traveling the world. I will try and find out about where he went so that I can visit his favorite places myself. He must have a record of his travels, somewhere in the house'.

21

It must have been a combination of total exhaustion, assisted by the sound of the waves breaking on the sandy beach. Mike slept better that night than he had in a very long time. In the morning he woke ravishingly hungry. He staggered into the kitchen and automatically looked in the fridge for inspiration. He decided against leftover pizza for breakfast.

Gathering all the nerve he could muster, he returned to the bedroom, climbed into the clothes that he had discarded on the floor last night. Heading for the kitchen, Mike grabbed the keys for the Jeep. They were as he had left them, laying on the kitchen table among the spread out legal paperwork. As he strapped himself into the driver's seat of the Jeep, he could see that there was a door control firmly mounted on the dash. He hit the control button and watched as the garage door slowly opened. The old garage door at his parent's house had to be manually lifted and closed. If his dad at all cared, he would have put in a power door unit to make it easier for his mom.

The jeep was a manual shift. Mike was grateful that he had learned to drive a classmate's manual shift pickup truck. This was so they could party and take turns drinking only a little, in order to be the designated driver.

Carefully backing out, he pushed the button and closed the door before driving off. As Mike left the driveway, he thought about the security system. He was unsure how to activate it when leaving the house via the garage. He made a mental note to search out the security system instructions. They must be somewhere in the house. Mike thought, 'Joshua was so organized, he must have a desk and file cabinet somewhere around here? I just need to explore more. It's strange that there is no desk in his bedroom or den'. Then he thought, 'I am still thinking about everything as belonging to Joshua. It's actually mine now. For sure, it will take me a while to get used to the idea'.

It was only one mile into the nearby village. Mike found a small local cafe. It had a sandwich board out front advertising home cooked breakfasts. Mike was ravishingly hungry. After a good hearty breakfast of ham and eggs with home fries, orange juice and three cups of coffee, he was ready to roll. He got directions to the nearest grocery store. One hour later Mike was back at the house with at least a basic supply of snack foods beer and breakfast items. He had also purchased an assortment of his favorite cold cuts, cheese slices and bread for sandwiches.

Across from the supermarket, Mike had realized that the bank was the one he needed to visit. It had a sign on the door denoting its hours of opening. As he expected, Mike would be able to deal with the banking issue first thing Monday morning. He decided to unpack the groceries and get settled in. He planned to call the bank and leave a message requesting an appointment as soon as they opened for the week. He needed to have proper ID as well as his copy of the will in hand, when he took care of the paperwork to allow access to funds. This was certainly necessary now. He had all but exhausted his pocket cash by treating himself to breakfast and buying the small grocery order. That cash was all that he had on hand. He always kept that money in pocket. Even a hint of it in his regular account would alert his dad that he had access to extra funds. He had no doubt that his dad would immediately reduce his living allowance in order to claw back any extra money that he made.

His thinking was, 'When Chandler gets here, he can help me get the kitchen up and running for supplies. He is better at that than I am. I've seen him helping his mother and sister prepare meals many times over the last two years. He will help me make up a list of what I need right away in order not to starve'.

Thinking about Chandler and his family, what Mike found amazing was that Chandler's dad also chipped in setting out condiments to add to the sandwich plates. He even helped set the table for the evening meals. Mike thought, 'It must feel great to do simple things like preparing meals, with your family all working together. That can never happen at my house. Dad just shows up to be served and god help mom if it is not on time and what he likes'.

Mike decided that his next chore should be setting up a bed for Chandler. Deep in the back of his mind he thought, 'If only I didn't need to set up a bed for him. My king size bed is so large. But he's not that way. It would probably tear our friendship apart if he found out that I am gay. Anyway, I have never taken the lead to lure anyone to bed. How would I even begin to do it? I have always let the men take charge of me and use me to satisfy their sexual needs'. Mike looked at the other two bedrooms. He decided that the one beside his would be best for Chandler. If he couldn't have him in his bed, at least he would be close by.

He went to the antique hall wardrobe and swung the door wide open. Selecting sheets and pillow cases that matched from the guest room shelf, he then reached for a cozy looking blanket. Having chosen this he decided on a comforter. The comforters were up on the top shelf. They were all large and bulky. Already loaded with linens, Mike leaned his weight to the left against the wardrobe frame. He used it as leverage to wrestle the heavy thickness from the shelf.

22

While in the process of doing this, Mike heard a loud clicking sound. He stood there completely startled. As the comforter fell into his arms, the entire large shelving unit swung inward, revealing a carpeted staircase. Peering up the stairs, Mike realized that he was overloaded with bedding. He swung around, crossed the hallway and tossed it all onto the bed in the second bedroom.

Mike returned to the hidden stairs and slowly walked up. Right from the bottom step it was clearly evident. He was not climbing up to an unfinished attic. Standing on the top step, Mike scanned the room. It was large and exquisitely furnished. To the right of the top of the stairs, there was a golden oak desk with a computer in the corner. The rest of the room was like a large den. It had a sofa with two matching chairs. They were facing a gigantic wall-mounted flat screen TV.

The wall to the far right of this grouping was filled with three sections of bookcases. Mike was drawn to these. He was curious, wondering what his uncle liked to read. He was pleased to find the first section filled with sea stories, both real and fictional. Propped between stands on the top of the bookcase, sat a large selection of DVDs. On close inspection, they turned out to be also sea-related documentaries and movies. The next unit was filled with classic literature and a large selection of glossy art books. These made Mike remember good times at the galleries, when he was small.

The last section of bookcase completely threw him. It was filled to bursting with gay literature. On top of this bookcase sat a large wire rack that was filled with DVDs of gay movies. It was clear that while some were gay classics; many others were explicit gay porn.

Stunned by this revelation, Mike crossed back over the room and sat at his uncle's desk. The desk was neat and organized, like the rest of the house. To its right sat a side wing containing a computer scanner and printer. Taped to the computer screen was a note giving Mike the password to gain access to the system. It also suggested that he change the password to one of his own choosing. Below this, sat, side by side, double drawer filing cabinets. They were built of the same rich oak as the desk. Sliding the top drawer of the desk open, Mike was shocked to see an envelope, with "Michael" boldly printed on the front. He drew out the contents and read,

Dear Michael

If you are reading this, I am happy. It means that you have overcome your father's tyranny. He would never have allowed you to come anywhere near my home.

You were not yet eleven when I last had a visit with you.

What you don't know is that your mother sent me constant notes about you and your progress. She also sent me many pieces of art that you produced in the summer programs.

I happily paid for these summer camps to avoid my brother finding out what they were about. I have no doubt that he would have refused you that activity. He would have also caused no amount of suffering and grief for you and your mom, if he found out that my money was involved. You will find the notes from your mother and all of your school report cards plus some of your art, in my file cabinet.

Look around on the side wall to the right of the TV. You will see a collage of your childhood art. I have always been very proud of you and your creative skills. I hope that you have been able to pursue your artistic training in spite of your father. A talent like yours should not be suppressed or wasted.

I can tell you now that watching you mount the stage to accept your high School diploma was one of the proudest moments of my life. It broke my heart that I could not stay and celebrate your achievement with you. Even though I knew that my bastard brother did not care enough to be there, the danger would have been too great for you and your mother, if he had found out that I was anywhere near the two of you.

I was never able to call or write back to your mother or contact you. If not for Jayne's involvement, things would have been impossible. Jayne was our savior. She helped your mother and me so much over the years. I was able to Email her any messages that I had for your mother. If your father ever discovered what your mother was doing for you behind his back, it would have been hell for her and for you. We could not have any direct contact. It was the only way that I could protect you from his wrath.

Perhaps I could have avoided all this mess. Who knows. It was probably a time bomb that would have exploded sooner or later. Unfortunately for us all, I slipped up and triggered it prematurely. I was feeling good about our last outing. That night your father was drunk and furious, in one of his usual uncontrollable rages. He told me that I needed to forget museums and galleries. He demanded that I take you to more manly things, like baseball and football games.

I guess I lost it. I told him that nothing would change. Mistakenly I know, in the heat of the moment, I lost my senses. I was so tired of tiptoeing around my bastard brother, just to be near you and your mom. I also told him that he should be grateful to have a brother like me. He demanded to know what I meant by that.

I really did it then. Your mother knew but I had never told your dad, knowing his attitude. I told him that I was gay. I stated that the day would come when you came out. I assured him not to worry, it would be good for you to have an uncle who can help and guide you along.

Your dad hit the wall. He screamed that you will never be gay; he would see to that. He then roughed me up and physically threw me out of the house, demanding that I never come back. I had no choice that night. I had brought on this storm. I scraped myself off your front walk. Thankfully nothing was broken. As you well know, bruises and scrapes heal.

During your dad's rage, your mother tried to intervene but he screamed her down. I was afraid that he was going to hit her. I later found out that he did hit her that night.

When I later contacted her through Jayne, I offered to rescue you both and bring you to the safety of my home. Your mom was too terrified. She was certain that if she did escape, your dad would search her out and kill all three of us.

Your mother is a wonderful, kind and loving person. She deserves a better life than my hateful brother has subjected her to. For your sake, I hope that you have come out and are happy.

I trust that you will make a good life for yourself and enjoy the comfort and security of what I have left you. I worked hard and invested carefully all of my life, it was all for you. You were the son that I always dreamed of having. If only my brother could have loved you half as much as I did, you would have had an easier go of it. I know that with your inheritance, you will now be in a position to make your dear mother's life happier and safer.

Love Uncle Joshua

In total shock, Michael stood and walked across the room. Yes there it was. How could he have missed it? An entire section of the sloped wall to the right of the TV was covered in a collage of his childhood art.

Mike sat across from his art work on an easy chair and wept. For the first time it was completely clear. He had lived so much of his young life enduring his father's tyranny. The strife and pain at home as well as the horrible loss of the uncle he so loved, was too much to keep bottled up inside. It had caused him to become a serious, unhappy and fearful person, someone who he did not wish to be.

Finally wiping his eyes dry, he rose from the chair. He realized that he was now looking beyond the office corner. Immediately across from the top of the stairs, there was a double set of doors. He assumed that he was looking at the opening for the unfinished portion of the attic, or a storage closet.

Carefully opening these double doors wide, he was frozen by what he saw. It was a large room totally decorated as a gay party room. It contained toys and equipment that one could only imagine.

Stepping forward, Mike walked around and examined everything. It was like walking through an exhibit of a fantasy gay sex haven. On the far side of the room, there was a wide opening rather than a door. Beyond the opening he could see a large bathroom area. It was fully covered in beautiful white ceramic wall tile, with a butterscotch streaked marble floor. It matched the marble floor in the master bath. More lighter veined marble covered the back wall, ending just inches shy of the ceiling.

There was a long trough-like sink with three sets of taps, as well as a toilet, bidet and wall mounted urinal. These were all installed along one wall, completely open to the entire room.

The entire back third of the room was a large shower. This was separated from the room by two sections of thick, curved clear plate glass. They were attached to the side walls leaving a large center gap. The combination of the curved glass dividers and the center open space afforded a clear line of vision for all present to see. What was taking place in either direction would be the entertainment for everyone to enjoy.

In the shower area there were four separately controlled shower stations, complete with ceiling mounted rain nozzles. They all came from a stainless steel post. This was mounted floor to ceiling in the center of the slightly sloped marble-covered floor. Four men could shower at the same time, all facing each other. The sight and thought of this made Mike's breath begin to shorten and his manhood start to quiver.

104 Nino Balistreri

23

The fantasy picture that was evolving in Mike's mind was abruptly cut short by hearing the doorbell chime from below. Mike rushed back through to the den and down the stairs. He firmly closed the linen wardrobe door and rushed to the front of the house.

Swinging the front door wide open, he found his roommate Chandler standing there, with an overflowing gym bag. Looking down at the mess of clothing at his feet, Chandler admitted, "Man, there was such an argument going on, while I was eating my breakfast early this morning. This time it was about a white carpet to be rolled out along the church isle ahead of my sis. Mom saw it on a soap opera wedding, no less, and had to have it. She went and reserved it without telling dad. He was totally freaking at yet another thousand dollars down the drain. I couldn't take it anymore. I grabbed my things and ran for the door. As I passed them I just yelled, "Mike needs me to help him. I'll see you later. I literally ran for my car, before they could ask questions, or even register what I said.

"Thank god I have my own wheels. If you had not rescued me, I would have been stranded in the middle of that war for a whole week. I would've arrived back at the dorm, a brain dead zombie."

They both had a hearty laugh over this statement. Mike led Chandler in and directed him to the guest room, so that he could dump his bursting bag on the floor. Looking around, Chandler exclaimed, "O M G Mike, is this it? Is this what you inherited?"

Nodding, Mike confirmed it. "Yup I am now a home owner and much more." He added, "I picked up a few breakfast and lunch things and a twelve pack of beer this morning, but not much else. I'll drive us into town later. We can have an early supper in town and buy more food."

It took a couple of minutes, before what Mike said sank in. Chandler asked, "You will drive me to town? Does this mean that you now also have a set of wheels? It makes sense that if your uncle had such a fine house, he would also be able to afford a car. I just hope that it's not an old gas-guzzler like mine.

Smiling Mike said, "Follow me." Mike led Chandler through to the kitchen. Opening the far door he stepped into the darkness, then to one side. Throwing the lights on, he caught Chandler perched in a stunned state on the door sill. The sight before him was completely shocking.

Finally Chandler stepped down into the garage and ever so slowly almost tiptoed around the vehicles. He was totally awed. He dared not even touch one of the vehicles for fear that it would disappear, like a mirage in the desert. Completing his inspection he turned to Mike, "I can't believe this; it is just too amazing. At our age we can only fantasize of some day owning rolling stock like this. The Jeep is a hot wheel dream. That sports car is far beyond a dream." Now truly hyper and excited Chandler exclaimed, "O M G! Have you tried them out, is it allowed?"

Chuckling, Mike replied, "It is allowed; they are officially mine. Each vehicle had an envelope on the front seat. My uncle signed the ownership papers over to me, as well as arranging the insurance policies. I just need to have it all officially processed. There was a note included reminding me to do it all right away, but I can drive them now. I plan to go to the auto registry office first thing on Monday to complete the final paperwork. But first I'll do some business at the bank. I need access to usable cash that my father can't trace. My mad money from the modeling job has all but run out. I don't dare risk touching my school expense account."

Chandler asked, "Why is that? Are you short of cash? I can get some from my account if we go to a bank machine. Or if you need more than my daily limit, I can give you a check to deposit. But why can't your father know about using cash. Does he not know that you are here and have inherited a house?"

There was no longer a need for secrecy. At least not with Chandler. Mike more than trusted him. His heart painfully ached for want that Chandler would be much more than just a friend. He yearned to be intimate with Chandler. Mike led Chandler out through the patio doors and they sat on the edge of the deck facing the ocean. They both removed their socks and shoes in order to run their bare feet through the sand. Mike explained the will situation in detail, in order to bring Chandler up to speed on what had happened.

Hearing about the scene at the lawyers and Mike's dad trying to swindle him out of his inheritance, left Chandler in shock. He told Mike, "Man, I am so sorry about that. It's been evident to me just in the short visits that I've had to your home, that things were much less than kosher. But I had no idea it was that bad. I am sorry to hear how you were raised. There should be a special hard labor prison for wife and child beaters. My parents are so loving towards each other. When my sister and I were small we thought that it was so icky the way that they carried on in front of us. My dad is such a softy. I can't even visualize what it would be like, if he ever raised a hand against either me or my mom."

Mike assured Chandler, "Don't worry, my dad's abuse and cruel life style are about to crash at full speed, right into a wall. He doesn't know it yet but he soon will. I am planning one last special visit home in the next two weeks. Don't be surprised if the end result of that visit is a long overdue divorce. My mother has suffered enough, both mentally and physically, at his hands. When I get through with him, he will never again leave either of us emotionally bruised and physically beaten!"

Looking around himself, Mike exclaimed, "My uncle obviously did not die suddenly. He left everything in perfect order so that I would have no hassles here. My only hassle will be when I go home for my last visit, but you can be assured, I will be more than well prepared to deal with that scene by the time it happens.

"To further answer your earlier question, I did drive the jeep this morning. It's a blast to ride around in. I had breakfast in town and bought some beer and a few groceries. I can't wait to take it for a spin with the top peeled off. I think that I'll hold off on the Miata for a couple of days. At least, until I get to town and do the paperwork to transfer the ownership. From what I can see, it's a pretty high-tech machine. I'm sure that I will need to study the manual before I even try to start it, or attempt to move the roof."

Hearing this statement, Chandler almost shrieked, "O M G! You mean the roof comes off? It's so solid looking. I thought it was a hard top coup. It must take two people to lift it off, it looks so heavy. Then what do you do if the roof is here and you get caught in the rain?"

Laughing Mike filled him in, "No, you don't lift it off. I haven't tried it, not until I read the manual, but I have seen it on line. One of my classmates was orgasmic over the U tube video when it came out. The roof is completely automated. It lifts folds and slips behind the seats, leaving only a wide, smart roll bar visible."

Chandler exclaimed, "Oh God, a convertible sports car with a power hard top roof. If I faint watching it lower, just lay me across the hood and I'll be happy."

They both laughed at this statement. But hidden behind his laugh, Mike thought, 'Oh man, I would love to lay you over the hood and do unspeakable things with your hot bod. If only I could!'

Leading a now totally awestruck Chandler from the deck, Mike then gave him a complete tour of the house. He carefully avoided the antique wardrobe. It was now closed up tight, his secret sealed away in the hall. Mike thought, 'This part of me will definitely have to stay hidden, for now at least'. He was terrified to share it with Chandler, for fear of destroying their close friendship. Mike was positive that no straight roommate would ever feel comfortable lounging around a dorm room nearly and often naked, with a 'Gay boy'.

Towards the end of the afternoon, Chandler helped Mike to roll back the canvas roof and strap it down. Then they jumped into the Jeep and headed for town. Zipping along in the open air, riding in an open Jeep was amazing. No two guys ever felt so cool and sexy at the same time. Two hours later, after touring around the area and searching out the nearby public beach, they stopped at a seafood pub. A tankard of cold draft and fish burger platters later, they headed for the grocery store.

Mike decided, knowing that he was running low on cash, "Let's get some extra lunch stuff, whatever you like, plus lots of snack foods and an extra dozen beer. That will break me till I get to the bank tomorrow. I already have breakfast supplies and a few other things in the fridge. We are only here for the rest of next week. There is no point in buying groceries for meals. It's my treat; we'll eat our dinners out for the next six days."

Chandler had no problem with this plan. He readily agreed, commenting, "Sounds great to me. It certainly beats the cafeteria food back at the residence. I'm not missing meals at home either. Mom and sis are totally wrapped up in the, as I call it, "The wedding wars". Since I got home we've been eating nothing but crap leftovers that mom put down in the freezer. She usually cooks my favorite foods when I am home for a break. No such luck this time."

Then, having second thoughts, Chandler suggested, "Mike, you had better let me pay for our meals out. My budget can stand one week of it. You are probably stressed enough, trying to figure out how to support all of this new grand lifestyle of yours! The insurance on two high-end vehicles alone must be gargantuan. I know what it costs to run and insure my old beast and it has little actual replacement value.

"If what you need to float all of this is more than I have in savings, I can hit my dad up for funds. He is good for it, I am sure of it. He will be more than happy to help you out. All I have to do is ask him and that goes for Mom too. With my parents help, you can survive till you graduate and start earning your own money."

Mike assured Chandler, "Please don't fret, over the money thing. I am actually OK. Uncle Joshua left enough to more than cover my new expenses. It is just a matter of completing all of the legal matters. Thank you for treating me to supper tonight. But tomorrow morning I will go to the bank here on the Cape and sign the transfers so I have immediate funds. Then next week, I just have to arrange a meeting with the stock brokers in Boston to go over and transfer ownership of Joshua's investment portfolio. I have an awful lot to learn about every aspect of my new existence."

Hearing the terms, "Stock Brokers" and "investment portfolio" left Chandler speechless. He could not imagine what a portfolio looked like. He told Mike, "When my sister and I turned ten, Granddad gave us each an envelope containing ten shares in Walt Disney Studios. He told us that we now owned part of Disney World. We thought that this was way cool. To date, those ten shares make up my complete Portfolio. I know that Dad owns stocks I have sort of heard him talking to Mom about prospective companies, but being a poor student, I have never paid attention to the subject.

"I am just grateful that my parents planned for and can afford to pay the lion's share of my educational costs. It left my granddad's bursary free to mostly cover the extras. Affording gas and a generous supply of oil for my beast and beer money, is all that I invest in these days."

Realizing that Chandler was now off somewhere, deep in thought, Mike grabbed the opportunity to add, "But you have no idea what it means to me that you are so ready to risk what savings you have, to bail me out when I'm in trouble. You are truly a best friend in every sense. If it was not for your offer of generosity and help, I would be totally screwed and on my own. God knows, the only help that I could expect from my dad is to be robed blind and left penniless, totally dependent on his hateful whims. That bastard really believes that I will go to work for him after I graduate. He has plans to make money off my back. Hell will freeze over first!"

That evening they sat around, as always in their boxers. Mike put their favorite music on using his tablet play list and wireless speakers. It was a top rate set up, with excellent sound. He told Chandler. "I never take any of this home on his breaks. Dad would hit the wall and more, if he had any idea how much I spent on these electronics or where I got the money to purchase them." They chilled and talked college over several cans of beer and a giant family-size bag of chips.

During the evening, Mike thought, 'Thankfully, Chandler has not commented on the lack of a television in the living area'. There was a good sized wall mounted one across from the foot of the master bed. Mike wished he had the nerve to put a movie on and invite Chandler to lay in there with him. He told himself, 'Maybe later in the week, if I can only get up enough nerve to suggest it. I could choose a movie that was sexually explicit to possibly fuel things up'. Shaking his head he realized, 'Oh God who am I fooling. I'm just too terrified. I know that I could never do anything that risky. It would jeopardize our friendship. But it makes my balls ache just thinking the about possibility of lying next to Chandler on that big sexy bed'.

114 Nino Balistreri

24

The next morning Mike woke early. It had taken him quite a while the evening before to fall asleep. He could not help thinking about Chandler sleeping nearby, in the spare room. It was different now, in no way like his dorm existence. His new found freedom and security, was all too quickly propelling him fast forward. He was now driven to take charge of every aspect of his life. The thought of sneaking next door and then slipping into Chandler's bed, was painfully overwhelming.

Finally, in desperation to get some sleep, Mike had to use the always friendly grip of his right hand twice. With enough pressure off his balls, he could finally relax and slip into slumber. With the early morning light reflecting off the ocean and streaming into his room, Mike jumped into his boxers and headed for the kitchen. Looking around for inspiration, he made a mug of coffee using the single serve machine. As he walked past Chandler's open bedroom door he glanced in. Chandler was, as always, burrowed deep under the blankets. His boxers were on the floor beside the bed, as they always were in their dorm room. Mike sighed at seeing this familiar scene. He could only dream about how marvelous it would feel, to slip between the sheets and cuddle up to Chandler's naked body. Not to mention what he would like to do with that body, once it was within his grasp.

Chandler had straight short-cropped dark hair and the most beautiful coal black eyes. His naturally curled eyelashes were nothing short of sensual. He was slightly shorter and smaller in stature than Mike. He had an extremely neat firm and compact body. This was probably thanks to his obsession with playing Soccer. All that running on the field had given him trim muscular legs, a tight belly and the most amazing buns.

Taking every chance he could to watch Chandler's buns flex, as he padded around their dorm room naked, Mike could just imagine how hard and firm they would feel in his hands. Mike already knew from two years of sharing a room, that Chandler was not near as heavily hung as him. But his trim round firm ass was a more than erotic pleasure to look at. Every time Mike saw it bare, his balls involuntarily ached.

Mike had many times peeked through lidded eyes in the morning. He loved to catch Chandler hopping from bed with his morning wood. It stood out rocket straight from its beautiful nest of tight black pubes. Chandler always jumped into his boxers, to head for the dorm's can. It usually took a while before he returned each morning. Mike could not help but fantasize that he lingered in the toilet stall to pump off a load, in order to calm down his morning erection. He could not help but fantasize, 'If Chandler would only let me take care of his needs every morning'.

Mike also knew from experience, that Chandler loved to sleep in when he had late or no morning classes. Knowing this fact would give Mike a half hour or more to safely explore upstairs. He tiptoed down the carpeted hall and quietly opened the wardrobe. Stepping in, he pulled the outer door closed behind him. He almost slid the shelving unit back into place once he stepped through to the foot of the stairs, but had second thoughts about this. 'I had better not seal myself completely in, just in case I can't easily figure out how to release it from behind. I have to figure it out. That's all I need, to have Chandler open the cupboard looking for a towel or some other supply. The linen passage door needs to be kept hidden just like my sexuality, for now at least'.

Reaching the top of the stairs, Mike did not hear the outer wardrobe door as it quietly swung open again. It had not latched tight. He sat at his uncle's desk and started to look in the file drawer. Everything was clearly labeled with post it notes, to help him understand. Uncle Joshua did a thorough job in prepping things for him. Mike was saddened that he could not see his uncle, just one more time.

Mike was thankful to his mother for sneaking all of his school work and art to Joshua. He never knew that Joshua paid for all of his art camps. He thought that his mother had diverted the money from her tight household budget. It now made total sense that Joshua paid. Thinking back, 'It would have been impossible for Mom to embezzle that much money from her already tight grocery account and hide it from cheapo Dad'.

Mike knew that the tuition was high enough every summer in the early days and more so as his skill levels rose. Then there was the ever growing cost of the specialized art supplies. He now realized that she never told him where the money came from, in order to protect him from his father. A child would easily let something like that slip at the wrong moment, causing their whole castle too crumble.

Sitting at the desk with the papers spread before him, Mike mouthed out loud to himself, "I will never forgive Dad for what he did to his own brother. I will also never forgive him for terrorizing Mom all of these years. He had absolutely no right to raise me in a state of continual fear. I realize now that he is guilty of both wife, and child abuse. Your day will come dad and thanks to Uncle Joshua, it will be very very soon."

Mike's thoughts were now running wild, 'I am me now. I need no longer live in terror. I will never again fear or obey that bastard. I will also never again go out to look for older men to control and use me. I know now that it was all because of dad. He raised me to be dominated, just like he totally dominates Mom'.

Getting up from the desk, Mike walked over to the video shelf in the far corner. He was so absorbed in reading the gay novel and movie titles, he didn't hear Chandler pad barefoot up the carpeted stairs.

25

Chandler at first did not see Mike. He was basically behind him, in the near corner. He was instead drawn forward towards the open double doors. Wandering around, Chandler carefully inspected every inch of the play room. He ran a hand over the giant round bed that crowned the center of the room. The sling and wide padded sawhorse was amazing. He jumped up onto the sling, to see how it felt to lay there. He then straddled the saw horse. He bent forward, leaning his bare chest against the cool leather. His balls began to ache as he started to get hard. Chandler was in true fact fantasizing that Mike was riding the horse behind him, pressing against his ass. From there he examined the shower room with all its fittings. Stepping back from the play room into the den, Chandler was startled to come face to face with Mike.

Mike gasped, "I'm so sorry, I was going to tell you about this when I could. But I was afraid that you would be upset."

Suddenly, Mike's line of vision dropped a bit. Even from part way across the room, it was obvious. Chandler's hard on was standing as it did every morning, straight out. This time however, it was proudly protruding through the opening in his boxers.

Realizing where Mike was staring Chandler looked down exclaiming, "Oh fuck, I can't help it. This is all too erotic. Your uncle must have had some amazing parties up here."

Shocked, Mike replied, "But you do realize that he was gay? You wouldn't have liked that kind of party."

Walking towards Mike, Chandler signaled that they should sit in the easy chairs. Once settled, he confessed, "Mike, I can't go on like this. Almost two years of sleeping in the same room has been torture. I could not ever let on that I wanted you badly. Every night that I don't have early classes in the morning, I head for downtown. I always told you that I had a date. In truth, I actually go to the gay bar and look for guys to hook up with.

"I have never gone on a Friday or Saturday night though. Guys at the bar told me that someone my age from the university comes in on those nights. I didn't want to be outed, for fear of it getting back to you and freaking you out. On those nights I always did the nearest bath."

"They told me at the bar that the young guy from my university always arrives drunk and lets older men buy him more drinks. This allows them to take him home and do as they wish with his body. They told me that he is a total passive bottom who is only into daddies. Guys my age that I have hooked up with told me that it's a wasted effort even trying to get near him. I could never figure out who it could be. At one point, listening to his description, I somehow had the impression that it might be you, but I dismissed the idea. Mainly it was because of the total bottom part. It made absolutely no sense to me."

Afraid to look into Chandler's eyes, Mike confessed, "You guessed right. It was me, but it never will be again. I have lived my whole life under my father's tyranny. I believed that it was my place in this world to be controlled, used and commanded. I know that letting older guys take power over me, was just an extension of my bastard father's influence. The only benefit that I ever received from those sessions was to satisfy my need to be physically held by another human. I assure you. That part of my life has now totally ended."

Hearing this revelation, with a strange smile on his face, Chandler stood up, hard on and all. He addressed Mike, "Please stand up, Mike."

Unsure of what this was all about, Mike stood. They were now facing each other, clad in only their boxers. In a flash, Chandler reached out and drew Mike firmly into his arms. He gasped, exclaiming, "Oh god, I have wanted to feel your body hard up against mine since the first day that we met."

Realizing what he had just heard, Mike threw his arms around Chandler. They kissed passionately for the first time. Mike's body was now surging with newfound strength and confidence. Smiling, he broke the embrace. He grasped Chandler's hands and announced, "I surely hope that you are game, because this ex bottom intends to lead you into his den of iniquity. I will show you how I now perform, as a totally evolved and very horny new-born top."

Grinning wide, Chandler said, "Lead on, Sir Mike. You have no idea how game I am when it comes to you. I am yours and am anxious to be enlightened"

Arriving beside the round party bed, Mike instantly grabbed Chandler's Boxers and sent them to the floor. He pushed Chandler back onto the bed, then dropped his own boxers and leaped forward. The rest of the week was spent in the play room, as well as the master bed. Over and over, Mike and Chandler consummated their up to now hidden lust for each other.

First thing Monday morning, Mike went to town and completed the paperwork to transfer the vehicles to his name. Then he went to the bank and took care of the cash and savings accounts. The bank had been pre warned by the Boston lawyer's office and now Mike's phone message that he had arrived on the Cape.

When Mike inquired about the possibility of applying for a credit card, they all but fell over themselves to issue him a temporary card and order a proper one with his name embossed on it. They asked if Mike wanted to have the minimal payment taken from his account every month. He knew enough to be aware that they would charge him interest on any balance.

They also asked if his uncle's credit limit would be suitable for him. He told them that any limit that his uncle had would be fine for him. He requested that the full balance be paid on every statement date. Leaving the bank, Mike glanced at the numbers on the paperwork. He could not believe what he saw. Joshua had a monthly limit of thirty thousand dollars on his credit card.

Even though the currents were not yet summer warm, they enjoyed a fast plunge into Cape Cod Bay every afternoon that week.

The following Sunday evening they drove Chandler's car and the Sahara back to the Dorm. They would have to make do with sharing a single bed for the balance of term. They didn't see that as a problem; it was just for a few weeks. They were now permanently locked in each other's arms every night. After a hilarious tumble on the first night, they dragged the mattress off each bed and placed them on the floor side by side. There were no bruises or broken bones from their first cascade to the floor during sex. But there was no point in courting the disaster of broken bones so near the end of term.

26

The following week, Mike made a major decision regarding his college future. Because his marks were high and the spring term all but over, he planned to finish his year. also, during this time, he registered at the accompanying arts college for the fall term. Thanks to all of his summer art classes and a recommendation filed by his professor of art, Mike was able to slide into second year. Once this was all confirmed, Mike resigned as a model for the life form classes. At the same time, he assured his professor, "If you are ever stuck, I will always be happy to help out."

The arts college, as well as dorm rooms, had small one bedroom apartments for students that cohabited. Two mornings later, Mike made financial arrangements for one of these to be leased for the upcoming fall term. He decided that if it did not work out, for the following term he planned to rent a furnished student housing apartment off campus.

Once this last bit of arrangement was sorted out and signed for, he met Chandler in the cafeteria for lunch. Mike could not wait to fill Chandler in on his plans. "I've made all the arrangements for us. I want you to spend the whole summer with me at the Cape house. In the fall you can return to your own courses if you're happy with them, but I will not. I will be attending the arts college on the far side of the campus.

"I've reserved a one bedroom student apartment and paid for two parking spaces. I decided that the jeep is a perfect vehicle for me to drive while at college. We can drive the sports car on weekends and holidays for now. We just have to inform our parents to finalize things. I no longer have a need to hide who and what I am. I'm sure that my mom will have no problems with my life style. My dad will have big time problems with it. He can go and rot in hell where he belongs. I don't care."

Hearing this, Chandler hugged Mike tight. He exclaimed, "I love the new you. You are so strong and decisive. It excites me to have you this way. I hate making major decisions totally on my own. My parents don't get into conflict over advising me, but they can never agree on what direction is best. It took me a long time to figure out that how they acted, having different opinions, was just a trick to teach me to be strong and learn how to make my own decisions.

"Their personalities are so different and yet somehow, they seem to be completely in sync when any need for major decisions arise that involves them both. To have the man I love help to make decisions with me is so damned hot.

"Please repeat all of your plans, for both me and us again tonight. Especially elaborate on what plans you have for me at the Cape and in the play room. But please, do it while you are making love to me with that beautiful tool of yours."

Hearing this, Mike told Chandler, "I will be glad to ride you long and hard, while I tell you about my future plans for us tonight. But don't think for a minute that I will ever become my father! If we're to be a couple, it has to be an equal partnership. We talk, discuss and work out together what is best. That means not just for me, my needs, or my likes, but for the both of us together."

The following weekend, Mike and Chandler drove home to their parents. For Chandler at least, it was not a difficult or traumatic scene. Unknown to Mike, he had come out to his family during the previous Christmas break. At the time, his older sister was the most shocked. Both his future brother in law and his kid sister thought it was way cool. His parents basically always knew. They were more or less prepared when Chandler made his, 'Great Christmas Announcement'.

What surprised them this time was learning that he and Mike were now an item. They had never suspected that Mike was also gay. However Chandler did not tell them about Mike's new fortunes, or where they would be living when not at college. He decided, 'There will be plenty of occasions in the near future to bring this up. I'm sure that they expect things to go along as they have been'.

That weekend, Chandler had cause to feel so grateful and loving towards his parents. It worried him just knowing what hell Mike was surely going through. During the following two days, both his mom and dad sneaked in a private conversation with him. It was so funny, but at the same time lovingly wonderful. Like conspirators behind each other's back, his mom and dad gave Chandler the same message, "If you have any extra expenses in setting up house with Mike, don't forget to call me. You have only to sneak the word to me and I will slip you extra cash, whatever you need."

His mom had added, "I have enough stashes of dishes, pots and linens, to help you set up an apartment. Your sister refused any of my treasures. She wants to start out her married life with everything new. When your dad and I got married, we had no money. We were grateful for all the household goods and unwanted furniture that our combined families scrounged up for us. But I guess times have changed."

Chandler felt guilty having his parents offer financial aid, plus the donation of household goods while not telling them about Mike's lavish home and new financial security. But he had discussed this with Mike before leaving for home. They decided that they would go together to Chandler's parents in the next three weeks and tell all

Now feeling fully empowered, Mike replied, "You can forbid all you want 'til hell freezes over. I want nothing further from you. I have enough funds and investments to live any way that pleases me. I no longer have to live under your hateful rules, or in your hateful house. I am in control of my life now. You might as well learn to get used to it, because if you don't like it, you can simply go to hell. You can also relax that fist. If I ever witness it raised again in anger, I will call 911 fast and have you arrested."

Mike added, "But don't think for a minute, that you are going to drag Mom down into hell with you. You have done enough damage to her, both mentally and physically. So get used to the label. You are not a 'Real' man, you are a sick Abusive Man. You should hide your head in shame. I assure you that if need be, this entire community will know what you are guilty of. You are just damned lucky that our neighbors have kept quiet about your crimes for so many years. If Mom hadn't been so afraid of your violence, she would have had your sorry ass thrown into jail where it belongs years ago.

"So either fix it between you and Mom, or deal with her team of Boston lawyers. I will spare no expense to see that you are financially and socially ruined, rather than have Mom suffer at your hands one day longer."

Mike was not finished yet, "While we are at it I have other news. As of immediately I will no longer ever live under the tyranny of your hateful roof. I have my own home now on The Cape. Mom, Jane and her husband will always be welcome there, but you are definitely not. I am positive that you would not want to be there anyway; it was Joshua's home and now it's mine. I can finally admit to you now, because I don't give a damn if it belittles your stupid phony manhood. Uncle Joshua was right in telling you when I was ten, that I am gay.

"Furthermore, I will not be alone at the Cape house. I am setting up permanent housekeeping with Chandler, we are lovers."

Turning to his mother Mike gave her a kiss and a hug. "If you want to come with me now, it's OK. I'll send movers to get my clothes and personal effects. I don't want anything else from here."

Mike's dad was now as white as a ghost and in total shock. Seeing his state told Mike that he had finally made his point. He had now completed taking charge of his life. His dad was now sitting on a kitchen chair, with his mouth hanging open. Being speechless was a condition that neither Mike nor his mom had ever witnessed with this most violent man.

Mike placed his old cell phone on the table. He announced, "I no longer need this cheap crap phone. You can use it or cancel it. I would really appreciate it if you let my personal things be packed and shipped to me, at my expense of course. But if that costs you too much loss of control, then stuff it all up your ass. I am wealthy now and can replace anything I need."

With this statement, Mike marched across the kitchen. Before passing through the outer door, he handed his mother a card. "Here is my new cell number. If you see that he is getting violent or threatening, just call, I will pick you up immediately and have the police deal with him. I will not be too far away for the next two days. I have a suite at the old Inn downtown."

The following morning, his mother called, "Your dad has escaped to the office for a couple of hours. He has calmed down some and recovered a bit from the shock of yesterday. He hid in his den all night. I think he slept on the floor in his sleeping bag. This morning he appeared in the kitchen looking like hell. When he saw the determined look on my face, he realized that it was all for real. He begged me not to leave him. I have never experienced dealing with your dad this way. As you well know, fear and acceptance has never been his way of dealing with life's situations.

"It must be your new found strength, it has affected me too. I told him in no uncertain terms, that everything changes as of today. I warned him. If I even think that he is getting controlling or cruel again, I am calling 911 and will be out of here for good. He obviously believes me, because he was slinking around and totally silent for the first time since we were married.

"Mike, I have been so depressed and living in fear for so many years. It's a shock to think that like you, I am now in control. I can only hope that it works out and holds. I love you so much and also have love Chandler like a son. I hope for nothing but happiness for the two of you. If time heals wounds, I can only hope that some day you can both come home here. But, in the meantime, I will be more than happy to visit you and Chandler on the Cape."

28

Mike's mother blew him away with her next revelation. "I have a confession. You probably already know that I kept in close contact with Joshua. What you don't know is, you remember Jayne Wilson, our neighbor, who you always dropped your art work to?"

Mike admitted, "Yes of course I remember Jayne. I saw her when she was over at Christmas. I hope that she is OK?"

"Yes she is fine. The confession is, you remember that three or more times a year I helped Jane with the driving, so that she could visit with her elderly mother two states away. Well, Jayne is a great actor. She continually put on a performance for my sake to overcome your dad. I had no choice but to lie to you and your dad. The real story is, her mother died many years ago. In fact, Jane and I had many wonderful holidays every year, at your uncle's house on The Cape. If you look up on the top shelf in both spare bedroom closets, you will find large storage bins. One holds my Cape clothes and the other has Jayne's. I'm looking forward to our first visit with you and Chandler. Jayne and I have truly missed our regular visits to the Cape. Jayne will be so excited to get away again. She was never escaping like me, but she dearly loved Joshua and all his friends. George is also looking forward to visiting your home on the cape. He ever so kindly gave up the right to accompany us in order that he stay behind to afford you safety and support.

"We did spend almost a week with Joshua just before the end. By then he had full time nursing care. It was a horribly difficult and painful goodbye. Over the years I often wondered if I dared to take you with us, but Joshua agreed that it was just too dangerous. You would have loved visiting with him in his beautiful home. I am so sorry. You grew up never knowing what life could be like in a loving environment. But it would have been a time bomb waiting to explode if you ever slipped up and your dad found out."

Hearing this, Mike told his mother, "You have no idea how thankful I am to hear this. I've been feeling so bad that Uncle Joshua had died all alone and abandoned."

His mom had more to tell him, "There is one other thing. Text me well ahead of time so that I know when you and Chandler will be at the Cape house for your next weekend. Your Uncle Joshua was never alone. He has an amazing group of close friends. They are mostly gay couples who live in the area. They were constantly at his side through his illness, right to the very end. I have met them all and they are wonderful people. Through Jayne's internet, we keep in contact with each couple. I could never dare use my internet account because I lived in fear of your father spying on me. I will let Joshua's Cape family know when you will be in residence, so that they can meet you and Chandler.

"There is just one more thing. I named you Michael, after my father. He was a kind and loving man. Sadly, he died in a work accident, not long before you were born, so you never knew him. Your father forbade me to call you Michael. He said it was a sissy name. He forced me to call you Mike. It would please both me and Joshua so, if you would use your proper name. His friends will automatically call you Michael. It's the only name that they have ever heard Joshua call you."

138 Nino Balistreri

29

Mike thanked his mother again, "Now that you bring it up, I can just barely remember Joshua calling me Michael on our outings. I also recently met a Boston artist that Joshua collected. Once he realized who I was, he automatically called me Michael." Mike liked the sound of it, so he told his mom, "If it pleases you and Joshua, I will be Michael from now on. I'm sure that Chandler can easily get used to calling me that."

Two weeks later Michael sent a text to his mom. They had a two day break in classes coming up. It was added to a weekend, meant for finals studying. They would be on the Cape from late Friday night, till early Tuesday afternoon.

The following day his mom sent a text back, 'You can expect Joshua's friends around five Saturday afternoon. Whatever you do, 'DO NOT BUY OR PREPARE FOOD'! Just be sure that the bar up in the play room is well stocked and lots of ice is made.

Reading this, Michael wondered what his mom meant. There is no bar up in the play room that he had seen. Before heading to the

Cape for the weekend, Michael stopped at a liquor store and bought an assortment of spirits and mixes. He also picked up a mixed case of wine and two cases of beer.

Once settled in that evening, he and Chandler went up to the play room. They looked everywhere to be sure, but no hint of a bar could be found. Michael concluded that Uncle Joshua must have set up a portable bar on a table, when he had large gatherings. There was a good size plastic folding table hanging in the garage. He figured that it was used for a portable party bar when needed.

All of a sudden Michael had a revelation. Turning to Chandler he exclaimed, "O M G, Mom told me to be sure and stock the bar in the play room. It means that both she and Jayne know all about this room and what it contains!" Realizing the implications of this, Chandler started to giggle. Overcoming the shock, Michael joined in.

On Saturday morning they drove into the village for breakfast at their favorite cafe. On the way back to the house, Michael picked up two bags of ice. Well before five, Chandler had the kitchen island all set up with glasses and mixes, just like his dad always did back home. Searching in the dining room cabinets, Michael found a large silver ice bucket. He filled it and placed it in the center of the kitchen island, with the bar setup.

Sharp at five, the doorbell rang. Expecting this, Chandler and Michael went together to answer it. They were happily surprised to find six gay couples lined up on the walk. They were all carrying dishes heavily laden with food. All were ecstatic to finally meet Michael, and also Chandler.

They explained over drinks. Joshua had talked for so many years about his nephew and his accomplishments. He had proudly paraded every report card and piece of Michael's art before all to see. They had known from the start of Joshua's illness that his wish was that Michael would be the next occupant of the Cape house. They also knew that this could only happen, providing he could circumvent his abusive father. Joshua had made it known that his younger brother was a horrible and violent man. They also knew that his violence encompassed both his wife and Michael. Each and every one applauded Michael's announcement, that his mom and Jayne would soon be coming for a weekend.

They all admitted to being sworn to promising that they would look out for Michael if he managed to make it to the Cape. Joshua charged them with seeing that Michael was happy here and, to that end, they intended to do their best to honor Joshua's wishes.

By mid June, Michael and Chandler were ensconced at the Cape house for the summer season. Three days after they arrived, a cartage company delivered Michael's boxed up possessions from his parent's home. He piled most of it onto the garage shelving, only bringing the boxes marked clothing into the house. There was no rush to unpack and deal with the rest of his former life's baggage.

The following weekend, Michael invited Mac B for a visit. Mac was just a bit too tall and husky to fit into any of Joshua's dress clothes, but he was appreciative to take home sweaters, loose jackets and a good supply of casual wear. He admitted to Michael and Chandler, "I do try to dress the fashionable gay artist for my own openings and other gallery events. But really, when not in public view, I wear any old thing that I have. I will be honored to wear some of Joshua's finery."

Michael's new Cape friends had been kind enough to help him sort through and deal with Joshua's personal effects. The odd thing suited and fitted Chandler but because of his height and physique, Michael could only enjoy using assorted clothing accessories. Joshua did have a collection of smart and casual hats that surprisingly did fit both Michael and Chandler. At the back of the walk-in closet behind the row of neatly hung designer suits, Michael was surprised to find a wall safe. His helpers were amazed that he didn't know of its existence. They all knew about it.

One of them pulled a drawer out that still held Joshua's clothes. He reached against the back and retrieved a card, while telling Michael, "When Joshua was ill, he often had one of us get his watches and things from the safe. He wanted to organize it all for you. I'll show you how to open it. It's an electronic key pad. You can either use Joshua's code or input your own. The directions for changing the code are also here at the back of the drawer."

There had been so much to deal with, that Michael had not realized there was no jewelry in Joshua's bedroom. Once the safe was opened, he was truly amazed. There was a case filled with diamond, ruby, plain gold and emerald rings. In the case he found a note from Joshua.

I hope that these fit you. If not, they can be re-sized. You will find the name and address of my Boston jeweler on the back of this note. He is a real artist and completely trustworthy.

Another case held four expensive watches. Several other cases held cuff-links with matching studs for tuxedo wear. There was also an assortment of solid gold neck and wrist chains. Michael thought, 'This is amazing. Just when I think that I am grasping it all, more is revealed. These beautiful things, I will certainly wear with pride in remembrance of my Joshua. Once I am finished my education, I will buy clothing that is worthy of wearing such fine jewelry'.

30

In the week that followed, it was discovered that Chandler had never driven a standard vehicle. Michael had asked him drive home from a nearby dinner party because he had drunk a little more than Chandler. Over breakfast the following morning, Michael assured him, "This summer I'll give you lessons with the Jeep."

Chandler told him, "That will be fine, but I'm more than happy for you to drive me everywhere. Sitting on the passenger seat of the Jeep, I get a permanent hard on watching you. You grab that floor shift knob and work it back and forth, changing through the gears and stomping on the clutch. I nearly cream wishing it was my shift knob you were grabbing in the open air. And, oh, man, when I see that clutch rammed to the floor, I fantasize it is your rod ramming my ass. You are so hot and in total control."

Hearing this and realizing that Chandler was now breathing hard, Michael started to laugh. He swept Chandler up into his arms and carried him towards the bedroom. "Chores can wait a while. I need to do some heavy gear shifting. I have an idea; the ocean side deck is totally private. We'll go to town later and buy a double width lounger. I intend to start your official outdoor shifting lessons on that. It'll be your fault for making me so hot, if your ass is too sore to sit in the Jeep."

Chandler giggled and hugged tighter all the way to the bedroom, saying, "Yes sir, anything you say, sir. I will do my best to learn to shift in any way that pleases you, sir, especially in the open sea air."

In the days that followed, Michael and Chandler made having a swim in the warm Cape Cod Bay waters an integral part of their day. All of the adjoining properties had sand dunes topped with wild roses. If they stayed near the center of their own beach, no one could see that they entered the water naked for their daily swim.

They already had a calendar of engagements for dinners, at their new Cape friends' homes. Michael made a habit of driving the Miata on these occasions. On a daily basis he drove the Jeep. He was more comfortable with this vehicle. Michael was still feeling totally awed, every time he sat behind the sports car wheel and watched the hard top roof as it smoothly folded then slid in behind the back seat.

The first house guests they received in early July for a weekend, were Chandler's parents and his teenage sister. They were all awestruck when they toured the house. The late June wedding had gone off in more than grand style. That day, Michael sat proudly by Chandler's side for the whole affair. Chandler's older sister and her new husband were now on their honeymoon, touring Europe.

It was a good weekend for all. Saturday evening everyone roared with laughter at Chandler's finally relaxed and now quite inebriated father. Michael marveled at the fact that unlike his father, Chandler's father got continually happier and sillier as he consumed liquor. He actually turned into a total riot when he had more than a few drinks under his belt.

With a glass of Scotch in his hand and wavering on his feet as he looked the sports car over, he announced, "Michael, if Chandler doesn't treat you right, let me know. I will divorce my wife and marry you, as long as I get to drive this awesome car."

Laughing and wide eyed, having consumed her own multiple drinks, Chandler's mother retorted, "To hell you will. If Michael and that car are up for grabs, I will fight you for it. To hell with my company's policy of chauffeuring our clients around town. I'm getting tired of driving home buyers around in that damned over-sized SUV. If I had a car like this to drive, my clients could walk or drive themselves to the showings, I wouldn't give two hoots." The entire entourage broke into a gleeful roar over that statement.

Late that evening after everyone had turned in for the night, Michael and chandler heard strange sounds coming from above their bedroom. Both climbed from bed to investigate. At the last second, realizing that they were naked and not alone in the house, Michael suggested that they don robes.

Once out of their bedroom, they peered through the open door of Chandler's parents room. The bed had been slept in, but now it was empty. As they turned to go towards the living room, they realized that the hall wardrobe door was open. Standing at the door, they could see that the inner secret door was also open. Emitting from above they heard the distinct sounds of two people in the throws of lustful sex. They looked at each other in utter amazement.

Covering their mouths to hid the sounds of laughter, they quickly retreated to their bedroom and shut the door. In the privacy of their bedroom, Michael told Chandler, "If we ever had doubts about whether our moms knew about the sex play room, We now know for sure that they certainly do know what it is for."

Two weeks later, Michael's mom and Jayne arrived for a week's visit. She confided in Michael, "So far things have been going better at home. For the first time ever, I told your dad where Jayne and I would be for the week." She admitted, "For a few minutes your dad went so red at the news, I really thought that he was going to have a stroke. I just told him, "Get over it. I'll be spending a lot of time from now on at the Cape house. You should just hope and pray that before you die you might be welcome there. But don't think that either Michael or I are going to make it easy. You have a lot of forgiveness to earn, before your only son will ever want to set eyes on your sorry ass again.

"I then decided to spill it all. I told him, "You might as well know. Jayne and I have been enjoying our holidays at Joshua's for years now. Jayne's mother died many years ago. I used her as an excuse to get away several times a year and enjoy a much needed break from your tyranny. We were always welcomed with open arms at the home of your loving and most kind brother. His heart always overflowed with love for all. It's beyond me how he lived his life filled with love, while you, his biological brother, had nothing but hate in your heart.

"I left shortly after, not hearing a peep out of him. When I said goodbye he was still in too much shock to say a word. At this point, I'm really not sure why, but I do still love your dad in spite of everything. But if this new found strength of mine breaks us up or even kills him instead of curing him, so be it."

The following evening Michael and Chandler had all of their new friends over for a grand pot luck supper. It was a happy reunion for them to be with his mom and Jayne again. Many toasts were raised in remembrance of Joshua, their reunion with Michael's mom and Jayne, and in celebration of the new residents of the Cape house.

150 Nino Balistreri

31

As their first full summer month progressed on The Cape, Chandler was doing only fairly well with his driving lessons. He was now handling the jeep on the open road, with just a bit of hesitation. Heavy traffic and parking were still a major problem. He couldn't seem to grasp the finesse of delicate maneuvering, while coordinating pressure on the clutch. He kept panicking and stalling when close to another vehicle, or at any intersection that was heavy with traffic.

In spite of his lack of coordination, Michael liked the look of him behind the wheel of the Jeep. With this in mind, he made a decision. Chandlers' birthday was coming up in early August. Michael announced that he was having Chandler's old car cleaned up and repaired for his birthday gift. It was truly looking tired.

They dropped the elderly Buick off a week before the birthday. It was fifteen years old and looking sad. It had been a hand-me-down from Chandler's granddad when he had to stop driving. The fenders were showing major rust. The motor had a loud pinging noise and it spewed black fumes when Chandler accelerated fast. It also boasted a bulky body and an eight cylinder engine. It loved consuming vast amounts of gas and oil. Its appetite kept Chandler's budget strained.

As Chandler handed over his keys, Michael told the service manager with a wink that Chandler didn't see, "We'll return next Thursday morning to pick it up. I hope that the repairs don't cost too much?"

The morning of Chandler's birthday, Michael drove them to town. They enjoyed a celebration breakfast at their now favorite home cooking cafe. After breakfast they proceeded over to the dealership to pick up the repaired Buick. At the service department counter, the Manager kept a straight face when he told Chandler, "We had to do extensive work to your car. It was in much worse shape than we had originally expected. I hope that you're pleased with the results."

He then picked up the phone and requested that the car be brought around. In no time, a metallic tan colored Jeep pulled up. It was almost identical to Michael's, canvas top and all. It had a giant red bow mounted to the roof roll-bar. The service manager handed Chandler an envelope, "Here is your car. I hope that you are pleased with the results; it's been through quite a transformation, and oh, by the way, Happy Birthday."

Chandler was in such shock, Michael had to take his hand and lead him out the door, then physically help him into the driver's seat.

He told Chandler, "You look so good driving my Jeep, I decided that you needed one of your own. You'll have no problem driving this one in the city; it's an automatic." Chandler was dumbfounded. All that he could do was jump from the seat and give Michael a big hug and kiss.

That evening they had a pot luck party to celebrate the birthday boy, with all of their new friends in attendance. Chandler was besides himself with excitement. All of their Cape friends had known about the present. Michael had it parked in front of the house with the big bow attached so everyone could admire it as they arrived. Chandler had great fun that evening, but he could not wait till everyone left. He intended to thank Michael over and over again that night, up in the play room.

32

During the last week of August, a happy Michael and Chandler moved into the college residence. The apartments were basically furnished and equipped. Michael decided that anything extra that they needed should be purchased. He didn't want to start hauling items back and forth from the Cape house to the apartment. The following weekend they visited Chandler's parents. Chandler's mom took great pleasure in going through all her bins of stored treasures to let them choose anything they wanted for their tiny student apartment. Their needs were few while at school. Some casual clothes, bedding, towels, food, beer and lots of sex was all that they required.

The apartment worked out well. The treasures from Chandler's mom set them up nicely for linens and kitchen supplies. It was actually situated half way between the two campuses. After talking it over, they decided to maintain the cafeteria plan for at least the first term and only stock light foods and snacks in their little kitchenette. They drove down to the Cape house on most weekends.

Time had to be spent studying, so other than meeting friends for lunches or early suppers in town, they didn't do any actual partying or entertaining. Up in the attic den, a large window overlooked the beach and ocean. It was a perfect place to set up a temporary studio. Michael laid down a tarp to protect the carpeting. He set up an easel along with the folding table from the garage. On nice summer days, he intended to paint out on the deck.

For Thanksgiving, they spent four days at Chandler's parents. Michael marveled at the great feast. Chandler's mom, assisted by him, his dad and sister worked diligently in the kitchen. Michael helped his new brother-in-law set up and dress the vast table that would seat them all, as well as several neighborhood friends. This was a totally new experience for Michael. Hosting a lavish thanksgiving with family and friends could never happen in his parents' home. His dad would not wish to be that social, nor would he agree to, 'Waste all that money' on a lavish feast.

They were invited to also spend Christmas. Once back at their apartment, they discussed the plan for Christmas. It was decided that they would visit Chandler's parents for just three days over Christmas itself, but they would then head for the Cape. That way they would be able to host all of their new friends for either New Years Eve or day, depending on everyone's schedule.

Michael also called his mother and invited her and Jayne down to the Cape, if they were able to get away. In the end they had no company staying over, but a grand New Year's Eve was spent at friends on the Cape. On New Year's Day, they hosted a pot luck feast with many of their Cape friends and even some of their friends' visiting family members. Michael truly enjoyed the friend/family mix. He only wished that he had been born into a happy, loving and accepting family group.

By spring break of the first year of Art College, Michael was surging forward in his creative work. His professor encouraged him to paint all summer on the Cape. He promised Michael, "I'll schedule you in for a showing at the student campus gallery in November. By then you'll be ready to start getting feedback on your work." Michael promised himself to book hotel suites for his mom, Jayne and George, plus Chandler's parents and sister, so that they could all attend his opening.

By the end of the first month of the fall term, it was obvious that they were barely using one Jeep. One block away there was a large garage facility. Michael arranged for a closed heated garage, to keep Chandler's jeep dry and warm. It was not needed on a daily basis.

On their next weekend at the Cape, they drove both Jeeps down. On Sunday, they left Michael's behind, nestled in the garage, beside the sports car. One of the garage cabinets revealed custom cloth covers to protect the vehicles from dust. Even though the garage was spotless, Michael figured that his uncle would slipcover the vehicles when he jetted away for a vacation. They drove back to the campus on Sunday afternoon in just one vehicle. Chandler's Jeep would be best suited for navigating city traffic and of course being automatic, was easiest for him to drive.

During the previous summer Chandler also made a major decision with Michael's encouragement. He dropped out of accounting and registered in the School of Architecture. That career had always been his dream, but because of his high grades and natural aptitude for math, he had been lured by his parents into the surer financial field of accounting. After just the fall term, it was obvious that he had made a good decision. Chandler's work was excellent and his grades were consistently high.

33

Two days after Christmas that year, they left Chandler's parents and headed for the Cape. It had been a new experience for Michael in the weeks before Christmas to accompany Chandler to the city stores and choose Christmas gifts for everyone. Michael also bought gifts for his mom, Jayne and George. He planned to give them when they came to visit right after Christmas.

All of their friends were invited for their first official New Year's Eve party at the Cape house. The Cape Cod gang all assured Michael, that Joshua's New Years parties always took place upstairs in the den and play room. Michael and Chandler were not sure about this, but agreed to have their friends help set it all up, 'Like it had always been done'.

Two days before New Year's Eve, four of their friends came over and helped to get the party room ready. During the party prep, Michael and Chandler looked on in wonderment as one friend slid the double doors wide that covered a large closet shelving unit. The top shelf was filled with wine, beer and drink glasses. Below that, the next shelf held party dishes and a large supply of paper and utensils. The bottom two shelves were filled with plush towels, soaps and other supplies to service the bathroom and shower room. Then he grabbed the right side panel, released a hidden lever and slid the entire shelving unit behind the adjoining wall.

Amazingly, a full wet-bar setup appeared. Michael was once more shocked. The subject of a bar had not arisen up to this point. Michael had totally forgotten to ask his mom what she had meant, by suggesting a play room bar. Each time that she and Jayne were on the Cape, they entertained on the main floor and used the kitchen island as a bar. Chandler had also served drinks from the kitchen island, for every gay social gathering, just like his dad had always done at home.

They both marveled at the sight. Michael's mom was right; there actually is a bar in the play room. He had yet to discover this secret. The stock of liquor that was housed in the bar was extensive. There was also a large wine storage fridge. It was crammed full. Resting on the counter sat an ice making machine. It was plumbed to the bar sink. Below the counter they realized that it had a narrow dishwasher. It looked to be about two thirds the size of a regular kitchen machine. Michael was totally amazed that he had completely missed all of this. Now that it was exposed, the fridge gave off a smooth hum. Michael and Chandler were certain that they had never heard a motor sound in that area before.

Expressing their concerns about partying in the play room, their new friends assured them that Joshua always enjoyed any of his guests who wanted to sexually enjoy the facility. He just mostly hung in the den area, but occasionally he did make a sweep of the play area to mix and serve rounds of drinks.

They assured Michael that Joshua was in no way a prude. There were many occasions when he had invited 'a Friend from Boston' to be his guest. On these occasions he also joined in on every bit of the play room festivities. All of his friends hoped that Joshua would find a special guy to mate up with permanently. But that didn't seem to ever happen. Joshua made it clear to all; he hoped to have Michael living in his house some day. He believed that if he had a live in partner, it would make it awkward for Michael. Although he did admit to everyone time and again, that if he ever met 'The truly right one', he would not hesitate to go for it. He did have partners that lasted a while in his early days, but they had all long gone before most of the Cape crew came to know Joshua. This relieved Michael. He would have hated it, if he thought that his uncle led a lonely life because of him.

Jayne and his mom were not able to come over during this Christmas break. Things were going OK at home. The reason was, both had community, social and church commitments. Jayne had always been active in their community. It was a new experience for Michael's mom to be free enough to enjoy making friends, and taking an active part in both her church and the community that she lived in.

A long weekend was planned for everyone later in January. For the first time, Michael and Chandler planned to have Michael's mom, Jayne and George, as well as Chandler's parents all together. Michael insisted, "If we are now all family, our extended families should get to know each other."

Michael offered to host the gathering at a ski lodge North-West of Boston. His mom and Jayne both convinced him, they would rather be at the Cape with him and Chandler, as well as their gathering of close friends. To house everyone, Jayne and George slept in one guest room and Chandler's parents in the other. Chandler's sister bunked in on the living room sofa and Mike's mom slept upstairs on the den sofa that actually opened into another queen sized bed.

As the winter rolled on, Michael reveled in the joy of sharing his life with Chandler. He had never experienced such consistent love and happiness. Growing up, his feelings of love and happiness were short and fleeting. They were directly connected to his all too brief weekends with Uncle Joshua.

34

Just before the following spring break, Michael made a major decision. He looked through Joshua's ring case and made a choice. Then he invited all of their Cape friends over for a pot-luck during Spring Break week. He told them behind Chandler's back, that it was going to be a special occasion, a surprise for Chandler.

After a sumptuous pot-luck dinner, they all gathered in the large living room. Once everyone had drinks and were settled, Michael garnered every ones attention. He then walked over to Chandler and dropped on one knee. Facing him he announced, "Chandler, I have lusted after and loved you from the moment that we met. It's nothing short of a dream that you feel the same way about me. I want to always be with you. To prove my love, I want to marry you." Having said this he pulled a large diamond encrusted ring from his pocket, grabbed Chandler's left hand and slipped it onto his ring finger.

Chandler was in total shock. His eyes rolled back and he started to waver, on the verge of passing out. Michael had to jump to his feet and hold him tight so that he wouldn't crash to the floor. In short order, Chandler steadied and his eyes came back into focus. He flung his arms around Michael's neck and kissed him, "Yes, Michael, I will marry you!"

Everyone clapped and cheered. Then the two were pulled apart, so that they could be hugged and kissed in turn by everyone. Before the evening was over, a date was agreed on, for mid August. That would be the only weekend in the coming season when all of their friends were commitment and family free. Michael and Chandler insisted that they all be available to celebrate with them. The following day Michael called his mother. She was ecstatic at the news. They held off for a week and stopped for a night at Chandler's parents, to make the happy announcement.

That evening, after mixing a few rounds of celebratory drinks, Chandler's dad drunkenly announced, while grinning from ear to ear, "Well I guess that does it. I'm the loser in this deal. If Michael and Chandler are getting married, I will never get a chance to drive that car. Chandler will hog it to himself" Everyone laughed at this statement. Michael assured his future father-in-law, "We will be pleased to let you drive the Miata any time you visit us on the Cape."

This brought a round of applause from the entire room. Chandler's brother in law Rico and his now obviously pregnant sister were also in attendance. Stepping up to congratulate the boys, they too had an announcement. Chandler's sister Brenda quieted the room to get everyone's attention. "Rico and I have something to tell you all. I don't want to take away from my brother and Michael's special announcement. But we had planned to ask a favor this evening, while we were all here together. We have a most important job opening to offer Michael and Chandler. We would like you both to be Godparents. The reason that we need you both, is because there will be a godson for each of you to look out for." The whole room erupted in cheers. No one had known up to that point that twins were on the way.

Holding Michael's hand, Chandler spoke up, "Well, Sis, I was thinking that you had been hitting the pastry counter too often. But with twins coming, it certainly explains the shape of things."

Looking at a smiling and nodding Michael, Chandler went on. "I think that in this instance, I can speak for both of us. We will be honored to be godparents to your sons."

166 Nino Balistreri

35

July turned out to be a hectic month. Everyone pitched in to help with the wedding plans. A minister was arranged for from the Metropolitan Community Church in Boston. Chairs, tables, a wedding cake and a caterer were ordered. The wedding was planned to take place on the large ocean deck at the Cape house. Michael and Chandler could not think of a more beautiful setting.

The subject of renting a large pavilion tent had been proposed by the caterers. Michael and Chandler decided against this. If the weather turned out to be bad that day, their proximity to the open ocean would also make it unpleasant to be in a large flapping canvas pavilion. They decided that in a pinch, their home's living areas could be rearranged and cleared and the house set up for the occasion.

The day dawned comfortably warm, with just a gentle breeze blowing off the ocean waves. The blue sky had wispy puffs of clouds floating around, as if they had been custom ordered to decorate the sky for the occasion. The afternoon before, friends had helped them set up a trellis backdrop for the ceremony. A few hundred yards away on the main road there was a small motel. Michael rented rooms for Chandler's sister and her husband as well as a room for the minister, Mac B, Jayne and her husband and several friends of theirs from university. The guest rooms in their home would be for Michael's mom and Chandler's parents and his younger sister.

Because they were just two weeks away from returning to college, they had decided against a honeymoon trip. Being on the Cape in their beautiful home would be more than enough for now. They decided to explore Joshua's travel files that winter and plan an extensive tour of Europe to celebrate their college graduation. Both agreed that they had lots of time to travel in the future. There was no need to cram in a fast trip now.

Chandler walked down the aisle in a smart white tuxedo, with a powder blue shirt. He was accompanied by his father who wore his own black tux. Michael wore a medium blue tux with a white shirt. Michael and Chandler proudly wore studs and cuff-links from Joshua's jewelry box. Michael walked down the isle beaming, as he held the arm of his mother. She looked radiant in her new hairdo and ivory colored, floor length, designer gown. It was a present from Michael.

The ceremony went smoothly. Michael and Chandler had chosen matching wedding bands from Joshua's jeweler in Boston. After the preacher had them kiss and announced the newlyweds to the gathering, both turned to accept the applause from their loving followers. As Michael turned, he caught sight of what looked like a man peering from behind the distant bushes, down the beach way.

Glancing towards his mother, he could tell that she was also looking that way. She turned to Michael and nodded with a smile on her face. They both instinctively knew who the man was.

Both now accepted that, in time, wounds could have a chance to heal. His dad still had a lot of changing to cope with. A lifetime of aggressive and cruel behavior would not be an easy task to reverse. He had been seeing a psychiatrist as well as attending an anger management group at the local hospital's mental health clinic. The most important part of this major step was that he had sought out all of the professional help completely on his own.

If he kept treating his mom right, Michael could now accept what the future held. It would be in the distant future. But the day could likely come when his dad would also be welcome at the Cape house, and most importantly, into his and Chandler's life.

36

Six weeks after their wedding, a proud pair of Godfathers officiated at the local chapel near Chandler's parents home. One of the babies was named Wilson Chandler, after his paternal grandfather and Godfather. The other was named James Michael, after his maternal grandfather and new uncle/Godfather.

The elderly minister conducting the baptism seemed nervous through out the entire ceremony. He admitted later at the reception, "I'm sorry if I was a bit shaky today. This is the first time that I have conducted a baptism with a gay couple as Godparents. Please don't be offended, I do approve. It is just that I was afraid to say the wrong thing and upset you. The whole traditional ceremony is so ingrained into my mind after all of these years that I hardly think of the words. I'm like an old parrot just rhyming it all off." To his obvious relief, both Chandler and Michael assured the elderly parson that he had done a fine job.

Later that evening when Michael and Chandler were cuddling in bed in Chandler's old bedroom, it was obvious that Michael was deep in thought.

Chandler asked him, "You seem a long way away. Is there something on your mind other than ravishing me?"

Hugging him tight, Michael admitted, "Yes. What we went through today made me think a lot. We are young and certainly financially sound. I don't want to rush into this. But would you be willing to at least entertain the idea of either adopting, or possibly having a Surrogate baby from each of us.

"We would have to wait, at least till our university days are over and we get settled into careers. If you were working for a nearby architectural firm somewhere on the Cape, I could build a studio attached to our house, or really, wherever we decided to live. Your career will dictate the location. That way my schedule as a full time artist would be more flexible, when it comes to being around for our kids on a daily basis."

Chandler hugged him tight. "Actually, I was thinking along the same lines, when we held the babies at the church today. I just wanted to never let go of mine. But I am sure that sis would strongly object. A pair of babies that looked like you and me would be an incredible completion of our family. I truly am sure that Joshua would have more than loved to help bring up two beautiful grand nieces or nephews."

The end

About the author

Nino Balistreri was born and spent his younger years in Barrie Ontario. He attended high school in North Bay, Ontario. As a teen he lived with an aunt in Chicago for two years. He studied social work and lived in Toronto and Ottawa before his love of the ocean drew him to the East Coast. Being of Sicilian heritage and coming from the cold of Ontario, Nino has a love of tropical climes. He enjoys his winter writing time in both Florida and Hawaii.

As a child Nino felt removed from both his family and the religious society that taught and abused him. His only safe place in life was to create a fantasy world where he could be nurtured and unconditionally loved. Constantly escaping to his own world gave him a reason to live. It helped him to survive till adulthood.

As an adult Nino was famous for entertaining his friends with never-ending tales. He could expand the simplest of happenings into a too lengthy account. By his mid forties Nino realized that his own fantasies could be translated into fiction and adventure stories.

Thanks to professional tutoring, he was able to format his ideas into print. His first three books, Death's Secret, Anchorage of Gold and Danger Cave were published by Create Space which became Kindle Publishing. He also contributed to Salt and Wild a compilation of Shelburne NS writers. It was published by Boularderie Island Press. A Florida based detective novel titled Lauderdale Tales is now available along with all of his books on Amazon Books as well as online with Cole's, Indigo and Chapters. This publication of Becoming Michael will be followed by a seven-part vampire series titled Blood Lust.

Nino belongs to The Writers Federation of Nova Scotia and when in Florida attends Pine Island Writers.